Acclaim for Howard Owen's

Littlejohn

"*Littlejohn* is a beautifully written novel, and Howard Owen has created a character as fully rounded in his quirks and imperfections, his quiet determination and bravery, as any in recent fiction." — *Washington Post*

"A sparkling story of a life lived, if not well, then fully.... Howard Owen joins that distinguished stable of writers—Jill McCorkle, Tim McLaurin—whose literary geography encompasses the region bordered by Ashpole and Barbeque, Shoe Heel and Colly." — *Fayetteville* (N.C.) *Observer*

"Howard Owen's fine novel unfolds with grace and subtle energy." — *Charlotte Observer*

"[Owen] not only has a felicitous way of writing but treats his characters with simple, lovely tenderness that is both subtle and heartfelt." — *Detroit Free Press*

"You don't want to turn the last page, end it, and have to leave this old man." — *Denver Post*

"[An] immensely moving tale of the human journey." — *Kansas City Star*

"Howard Owen is a gentle writer whose unassuming but first-rate novel catches you off guard, like a clap of thunder on a clear day." — *Entertainment Weekly*

"This compact, poetic first novel sneaks up on you and won't let you go.... In his quiet, colloquial heroic way, Littlejohn is a wonderful addition to the pantheon of American literary characters." — *Greensboro* (N.C.) *News & Record*

Books by Howard Owen

Fat Lightning
Littlejohn

Howard Owen

Littlejohn

Howard Owen was born and raised in Fayetteville, North Carolina. He is a graduate of the University of North Carolina at Chapel Hill, and is the sports editor of the *Richmond Times-Dispatch*. He lives in Midlothian, Virginia, with his wife, Karen.

HOWARD OWEN

Littlejohn

Vintage Contemporaries
Vintage Books
A Division of Random House, Inc.
New York

CELEBRATING

10

Years of

VINTAGE CONTEMPORARIES

FIRST VINTAGE CONTEMPORARIES EDITION, AUGUST 1994

Copyright © 1992 by Howard Owen

The Library of Congress has cataloged the Villard Books edition as follows:

Library of Congress Cataloging-in-Publication Data
Owen, Howard.
    Littlejohn/by Howard Owen.—1st ed.
    p.   cm.
    ISBN 0-679-42769-4
    I. Title.
  [PS3565.W552L58 1993b]
   813'.54—dc20   93-10068
Vintage ISBN: 0-679-75001-0

Author photograph © Deane Winegar

To the women of my life:
Karen Van Neste Owen
Roxie Bulla Owen
and Janice Owen Faircloth

Acknowledgments

Grateful appreciation goes to Martin and Judy Shepard of the Permanent Press for giving *Littlejohn* a chance; to Marcia Meisinger and the rest of the staff of the Book Nook for spreading the word; to Max Gartenberg for being a great agent; to Robert Merritt for good advice; to Karl and Penny Van Neste for the computer; to Bill Pahnelas for helping me get acquainted with it; to Sally Biel, Freeman V. Turley and Leslie T. Farrar for their support; to Deane Winegar for the photos; and to Diane Reverand, Jackie Deval, Beth Pearson, Alex Kuczynski and everyone else at Villard Books for helping make a dream come true. And, as always, to Karen.

Littlejohn

CHAPTER ONE

July 31

Somebody I know but can't make out is leading me down the old pine-straw-matted road to the millpond. The pine straw is slick as glass, and I keep slipping and falling in the hot sand. I hear that somebody keep saying, "Hurry up, Littlejohn, or you'll be late," but I can't get my legs to work right. I'm half crawling, half running toward the pond, and pin oak and pine branches keep hitting me upside the head.

Finally, I come to where the road runs out, and there's Lafe, waiting for me at the edge of the water, laying at that same old pine tree where it happened, except the tree looks like it's two hundred feet tall and six feet across, and this time, Lafe opens his eyes. There's a scar on his forehead, over his right eye, but he ain't dead.

Lafe don't say a solid word, just stands up, smiling that lopsided smile of his and brushing pine needles off his backside. He motions for me to follow him across the water, which don't seem peculiar. It's like them dreams where you can fly and all.

I always seem like I'm about fifty yards behind Lafe, and the water ain't getting any deeper as we walk out. Where, in real life, the millpond is maybe twelve feet deep in the middle, with nothing but boggy muck at the bottom of water dark as tea, we seem like we're just skimming across the surface now like two slick, flat river rocks.

And there, up ahead, is Momma and Daddy and them, all smiling and waving at me to beat the band. I can see Sara and Angora and Rose, not gone anymore. It looks like they're right smack in the middle of Maxwell's Millpond, which is at least half a mile across. I someway know, then, that they know about everything, all my secrets, and that everything is all right, that there ain't no shame in heaven.

But when I try to hurry across the water to meet them, my legs start getting heavy again, and I start to sinking. I look down, and underneath the surface of the water, it's turned to fire. Lafe is holding out his right hand, showing that same cockeyed grin, but I can't reach him, hard as I try. I'm going down in flames, and it's like one of them dreams where you know it's a dream even while you're in it. I'm trying to scream and watching myself trying to scream at the same time. For some reason, the fire ain't burning me, and off in the distance, I can hear this voice. It keeps getting louder, so that finally I can make it out . . .

CHAPTER TWO

August 8

Take me now, Jesus.

Georgia and Justin have packed up her blue Honda hatch-back, we've talked about whether the tires have enough air and when was the last time she checked the oil, and I know they're ready to put miles between them and here. To tell you the truth, I'm ready to get the good-byes over with, too.

I love them both to death, but I am wore out. And besides, I got things to do.

I hug Georgia, amazed all over again at how bony she is, at how much sharper she feels than when she was married and Justin was little. She tells me to take care of myself, and to do what Dr. McNair says, then lowers herself into the driver's seat. I walk around to the other side, feeling the sand that bunches up in the middle of the driveway give underneath my feet, and hug Justin, even though he'd probably rather of shook hands. The scars on his face have healed up real good. I remember that I didn't give them the beans I picked this morning, before it faired off and turned hot again, but they tell me to keep them. Georgia starts up the car on the third try, and I know the look of relief on her face is from not having to go through all the good-byes again, not because she can't wait to see her daddy's ugly face in the rearview mirror.

They back down the drive and head out the old rut road, trails of dust behind them almost covering their little car. Then they go over the top of the sandhill and dip down the other side, toward the paved highway, their brake lights coming on just before they disappear.

I turn around to go inside before they can come into sight again, headed north. Never have been able to watch people leave.

Back up the brick steps to the screen porch now, taking it real slow. Don't want any broken hips today. Weatherman said it would be 98 degrees after the sun came out, so to be sure it'll be over 100 where I'm headed. Maybe a lot more than that. Least I haven't lost my sense of humor.

The screen door sings as it bangs shut behind me, and I go into the kitchen to get the truck keys. But they ain't on the counter, nor on the porch table, nor in the overalls I had on yesterday. Then I remember the extra set Georgia had made for me, with the magnet on them so they could be stuck to the underside of the truck, after I'd lost a couple of pair.

When I get to the truck, though, there's the keys I was looking for, right there in the ignition from when I went to the store yesterday.

I crank up the old pickup, same one I've had since 1965. The odometer says 39997.4. If I took the paved road today, we'd crack 40,000. The seat's so hot I can't hardly sit, and it burns my hand to crank the window down.

I turn left, away from the paved road, at the end of the circle driveway, past the knobby old crepe myrtles me and Lafe planted so long ago. It's hard to keep it in the ruts, wrestling this old powerless steering wheel in and out of the sand as we go past the bleached-out barns on the right and the rented hayfields and Kenny's little garden on the left. The sun is just beating down; must be about one o'clock. When it reflects off this white sand, it makes it even harder to see. I think about the cataract operation I hope I won't have to have now.

On the left, a quarter mile from home, is Rennie's old house, nothing but fat-lightnin' ruins now. It's been awhile since I've been over the bridge that crosses Lock's Branch, and I wonder if it'll hold this old truck and me.

On past the tenant house, we dip down into the swamp, the rut road dividing fields Daddy and them cleared not long after he come home from the Civil War. You can smell things growing down here. Mackey Bryant's boy leases the swamp acres for beans and corn now and takes care of the strawberry business. It's good, rich land; never planted no tobacco down here. To the left is the little hill with our family cemetery on it, where Momma and Daddy and Lafe and them are buried, and next to that is the Rock of Ages.

Up ahead, a straight line of trees crisscrosses the road. That's the branch, where my land ends. Beyond that is the Blue Sandhills.

Just shy of the bridge, I stop the pickup and try to think when was the last time we replaced it. It was 1955 or '56, I reckon, because Georgia was in the third grade. Miss Louise Hornwright, her teacher, had supper with us, and she wanted to see the new bridge that Lex and me had built, that Georgia told her about, so me and Sara and Georgia and Miss Hornwright got into our green 1952 Chevrolet sedan and drove down here to see it. I suspect Miss Hornwright was a little let down over such a puny bridge, no railing or anything.

I let myself down out of the pickup and walk up the little rise. Down in the branch, there's not enough water to drown a ant. A big old garden spider, all yellow and black, has spun her web across the branch twenty feet away. All the slats seem like they're solid. I punch at them with my cane and they don't seem to give.

There's beer cans all over the place here, and in the bushes I spy something that turns out to be a pair of girl's underpants. No wonder there's so much traffic going past the house at night. I can't get that sorry deputy sheriff, Jake Godbold's nephew, to go down and run them out. I think he's scared of the dark.

Back in the truck, I'm seeing spots from all the sun out here. I look at the sucker-bait watch Jenny got me for

Christmas and remember that it stopped last week. I never could remember to take it off when I'd go to pick peas and butter beans, and sweat got in it, I reckon. The truck starts and me and it get across all right, headed into the Blue Sandhills.

The road goes right up a little hill with sand whiter than any beach you've ever been to. I have to know the way by heart, because I can't see a blessed thing. The Blue Sandhills ain't really blue, of course, but from off a ways, especially on a day like this, they can be near-bout the color of this washed-out sky. I reckon it's the dark earth right under the surface that makes them look blue. Nothing amounts to much out here. There's scrub pines and pin oaks and brambles, all kind of stunted. It goes on like this most of the way to the ocean, forty miles away, with bays and pocosins wherever there's a dip, and Kinlaw's Hell right in the middle of it. They say the land's like this because a shooting star or something like that hit here fifty thousand years ago and changed it all around. I hope I never have to see it again.

It would of been easier, of course, to go out the way Georgia and Justin did, on McCain Road right into East Geddie, then two rights to the Ammon Road, which this trail I'm on will cross up ahead a little bit. But that same sorry Godbold boy that won't keep drunks out of my fields at night has told me he's going to give me a ticket if he catches me driving any farther than the Bi-Rite in East Geddie or the Geddie Presbyterian Church. Told me I was lucky to have a license a-tall, since I didn't seem to recognize stop signs. Talked to me like I was a young-un or something. The deputy knows I grocery shop on Monday and go to church on Wednesday night and Sunday, and this is Tuesday.

Littlejohn

I finally cross the Ammon Road, all humpbacked and gray like me, with one end headed toward Geddie and the other going deeper into the sandhills. There's no cars coming either way. A dog could sleep on this highway, if it could stand the heat. I drive across the road, picking up the same ruts on the other side, and head off for Maxwell's Millpond.

Here the land levels off a little bit, with the scrubby little pines and oaks not giving much shade a-tall. Nobody lives here now, but this used to be a logging road. There was a sawmill by the pond where folks worked and was given cabins to live in. There was a sawdust pile here that caught fire in 1933 and burned for twenty years. They finally hauled it away a truckload at a time. Everybody called it Yankees' Revenge, after the sawdust pile of my granddaddy's that Sherman's men set fire to.

Before the loggers, they used to tap these pine trees for turpentine. Somebody's always tried to find some kind of use for this sad old country back here. A few years ago, they tried to make Maxwell's Millpond into a resort, like White Lake. They built them a road in from the other side and sold a few lots. They drained all the tea-colored water out and tried to pump clear water in from the East Branch and the natural springs down here. It seemed like it was working for a while, but the old water come back like a bad penny, darker than ever, and Sandy Spring Lake is Maxwell's Millpond again.

Closer to the water, I cross a couple of fire lanes they built when the whole place like to of burnt up in 1955. Nearer the pond, the land gets a little boggy and more wild. Finally, the pickup breaks through some tree limbs and I get my first clear look at this place in more than thirty years. We was helping fight one of the fires in '55, and a forest service truck

11

brought us up here for water, to this very spot where Lafe died, where it all started, in 1922. Until now, once in sixty-six years was a-plenty for me.

There's still a sandy beach here, and from the beer cans and burnt places on the ground, folks still come here to raise Cain. There's cottonmouths here, unless somebody's killed them all, which I doubt, that'll get ill just seeing you. Not too far over is where the tram used to be. The woods still haven't growed back there all the way, so that if you're headed east from Geddie on Highway 47, just before you get to McNeil, you can look south and get a glimpse of the millpond through the brush, two miles off. They built the tram to haul lumber from the sawmill to the Campbell and Cool Spring Railroad line in McNeil. By the time Georgia was born, though, they had just about cut all the hardwoods and a lot of the pines around the pond, and they left the tracks to the scrap dealers and folks looking for crossties to line their driveways with. They say there's still pieces of track left in the hard-to-get-to places.

And there's the pine tree where Lafe lay, bigger now, to be sure, but not as big as it was in my dream, the one that got me here and the one I hope to Jesus will be the answer to my prayers.

"Lord," I prayed a hundred times, I know, "please show me the way. I can't keep on like this. One day I'll fall and break my hip and be like old man Jimmy Ezell, up there in that rest home with nothing but mean colored nurses letting me wet myself and worse, running Georgia broke. Or, worse yet, I'll get so simpleminded they'll have to put me away.

"But I can't do it myself, Lord. I ain't afraid to die, but

I still hold to that outside chance that you might forgive me, and that Lafe and Angora and Sara and Momma and Daddy and them can, when and if I ever see them again on that other shore. And if I killed myself, there wouldn't be no hope a-tall.''

Eight days ago, Jesus seemed to answer me. In the dream, Momma and Daddy and them was real as life, and I was walking across Maxwell's Millpond, just like Peter when Jesus told him to. Maybe if I'd of had faith enough, it wouldn't of been a dream.

But I didn't, and it was, and the voice I heard when I was sinking was just old Johnny McLamb with the WPCR morning report on my clock radio, and then I was awake.

While I was laying there on my back, listening to my old heart beat ragged and weak, Johnny said it would be 98 degrees if it faired off. And then he said something that made me feel like he was talking right at me, like he was part of the dream, too.

''But if you think it's hot in Port Campbell, folks, just be glad you're not in St. Louis, Missouri,'' he said. ''Yesterday, it was 104 in the shade there, assuming you could find any, and four people died from the heat. One of them, a fifty-eight-year-old woman, apparently wandered from her house, which didn't have air-conditioning, out to the banks of the Mississippi River, collapsed in the sun and died before anybody found her.''

Around here, they'd say that the monkey got her. Many's the time, out in the tobacco patch, I've seen Lafe or Lex or one of the Lockamy children look up from cropping, pale as a ghost, and say, ''I see them monkeys comin' over the trees there.'' And they'd go to the shade at the end of the field, up by the pump, where somebody'd wet a rag and put it on their head, and maybe we'd cut into the watermelons early.

And sometimes the monkey would sneak up on somebody, and they wouldn't get out of the sun in time. My cousin Bert Averett, she had a heatstroke so bad that she never could talk right again, or use her left arm and leg like she could before. Clarence Curry, he was in school with me, died of a heatstroke back in 1938 and a colored man died of it last summer over past Cool Springs.

So, if a fifty-eight-year-old woman in St. Louis, Missouri, can be got by the monkey, and if he can sneak up on men in their prime out cropping tobacco, couldn't he make short work of a eighty-two-year-old dirt farmer who comes to the millpond here in the middle of the Blue Sandhills on the hottest day of the year and dares him to do his worst? And if the monkey does get me, wouldn't it be like lightning? Wouldn't it be a act of God? And if You want me to go on living, I reckon You'll spare me, just like You did Shadrach, Meshach and Abednego in the fiery furnace. Although why You'd want to do a thing like that, only You would know.

So, I've just been waiting for Justin and Georgia to leave. And if they think I just didn't have the guts to stick it out, that's not the worst thing they could know. And this will make it so much easier on everybody. I feel right bad about the will, but it was the right thing to do, no matter how crazy folks might think it is. Besides, how much crazier is all this than some of the other stuff I've been doing here lately? Like forgetting all about that stop sign in East Geddie and near-bout getting run over by a log truck, although looking back, that might of been the best thing, long as the fella driving the truck didn't get hurt. Or leaving the burners on the stove turned on so much that I finally had to put a big sign on the inside of the kitchen door that says TURN OFF BURNERS.

The worst, though, was what happened at the Bi-Rite, in front of everybody. I don't make out a list like Sara used to, although I reckon I ought to. Once a week, I go down to the store in my truck and get what looks good to eat. The Army taught me how to cook right good, but one old man don't eat a whole lot, and my appetite ain't as good as it used to be. So, I was wandering down the aisle. I had just put two cans of Campbell's cream of chicken soup in my cart and was looking for the self-rising flour when I just blanked out. I couldn't quite remember what I was doing there. It had happened once or twice before, but never this bad, or this public, at least. I looked around, and there at the end of the aisle was the meat counter. It seemed like I recognized it, so I went that way.

When I got there, though, I somehow had it in my head that it was Mr. Allen Butler's store, which went out of business in 1961 and burnt to the ground two years later. I can remember asking the meat-counter man where Mr. Allen was, and when he looked as mixed up as me, I asked if they had any of that good souse meat that Franklin Junior Bradshaw sold to them. The Bi-Rite, of course, is way too uptown to carry souse meat or liver puddin' or anything like that most of the time, and Franklin Junior was run over and killed by his own tractor more than twenty years ago. Then I reckon I got kind of wild, and somebody must of called Jenny, my niece, because her and her husband, Harold McLaurin, come and got me and carried me home.

Later on, I could remember most of what happened, and it made me feel so bad that I couldn't go to church for two

Sundays, I was so ashamed. Jenny, bless her heart, brought me groceries, and Reverend Carter and a couple of the elders come by to see me, so that finally I got so I felt like I could stand to see people again.

I asked Jenny and them not to tell Georgia, but I expect they did anyhow. Everybody around here knows about it. It aggravates me the way people act like you're not even there sometimes if you're old. After my spell at the grocery store, it seemed like I could say something in the yard after church and folks would just smile like they was humoring me or something, or like they weren't quite sure what I said was right, since it was a crazy man saying it. Some of them have even talked to me about going to a rest home, but I told them the only home I expected to live in for the rest of my life was the one that my granddaddy built. I would sooner be dead all at once than die every day in some old folks' home, which is what I told that Miss Bulla from the Senior Citizens when she come to visit me.

So, I get out of the pickup, which is parked maybe fifty feet from the water. In the truck bed there's the little wood stool, a foot and a half high, that I made a long time ago to sit on picking butter beans in the swamp.

I prop my cane on the side of the pickup and lift the stool out, then tote it to the middle of the clearing, between the truck and Lafe's pine that stands right by the edge of the millpond.

I take off my straw hat and sit and wait, looking out across the pond. The haze is so bad that I can't hardly see the south shore. Nothing is moving—nary a bird, nor the wind through the trees, nor the water. The only noise out here now is the locusts, sounding like bacon frying in a spider. I can't even hear a mourning dove.

For some reason, I think back to Gruff, and something he said one time during a Redskins game. It was sometime during the early sixties, because that boy Snead from Wake Forest was Washington's quarterback, and Sonny Jurgensen was still with the Philadelphia Eagles, which is who the Redskins was playing that Sunday. Gruff had come up from Georgia to visit. Him and me was big Washington fans; that was all you could get on television down here or in Atlanta until Johnny Unitas come along and made the Colts good in the late fifties, so just about everybody that could stand to watch them lose week after week pulled for the Redskins. You could catch the Atlantic Coast Line excursion train from Port Campbell of a Sunday morning, about five A.M., get up to Washington in time to see the game, then come back, just about everybody dog drunk, and be home by midnight. Me and James Lassiter did it a couple of times. Now I hear you can't even get a ticket.

Anyhow, Gruff was sitting with me in the living room of mine and Sara's house, watching the Redskins play the Eagles. Sara was laying down, and Georgia was playing the piano in the sitting room down the hall. And the Redskins was winning, which was near-bout a miracle back then. Late in the game, when it seemed like there weren't any way even Washington could lose this one, old Sonny went to work. With almost no time left a-tall, he threw the ball to this little halfback, boy named McDonald, and he caught it and must of run past six Redskins, finally just easing into the end zone while the announcers went crazy. I can remember it better than some things that happened last week.

So, I'm just sitting there, gripping the easy-chair arms and about to have a stroke, when Gruff rears back and lets go with a "Goddamn son of a bitch goddamn choking son of a bitch goddamn Redskins bastards." Gruff always was a rough-talking fella, although I always felt like his cursing lacked a little imagination. He used to get in trouble with Momma all the time about it before he left home for good. Me, I could call a contrary mule a hee-hawwin', lop-eared, knuckle-headed, dog-meat strumpet and so on for ten minutes without taking the Lord's name in vain. I knew Georgia and Sara could hear every word of it, because they both got real still. And then Gruff just looks up toward the ceiling, just like he's looking right through that plunder room in the attic, right through the tin roof, right up to heaven, and he says in a real quiet voice, "Take me now, Jesus; take me now." Gruff scared me sometimes.

But that's the way my brain is going right now, come hell or high water. I have lived with it all this time, and there was always a reason to keep on going. Now, there ain't. Everybody's fine now. The loose ends are all tied up, and it'd be better for all involved if Littlejohn McCain just meets You and makes his peace.

So, with this boiling sun making my scalp tingle like it used to when Daddy would send me out back of the smokehouse on a cold dark night to fetch more stovewood, me not knowing when one of his hounds was going to jump me and make my heart stop, I can almost see that old monkey coming across Maxwell's Millpond, and Gruff's words come back to me, not as a curse but as a plea: Take me now, Jesus; take me now.

CHAPTER THREE

July 19

When I was a little girl, I used to love to go with Daddy to the Godwin Lumber Yard in McNeil. A man named Arch McMillan was the foreman there, and he was the designated giver of directions to East Geddie.

"Mr. Arch," I'd ask him, "has anybody got lost looking for East Geddie today?"

More than one tired, dazed farm-implement salesman or

insurance agent had pulled into the lumber yard after fool-ishly heading east from Geddie on Highway 47 looking for East Geddie. They'd travel past deserted sandhills and scrub pines, and a house now and then, and by the time they got to the lumber yard, after perhaps driving back and forth two or three times looking for the nonexistent side road, Arch McMillan was ready for them. They were his prime source of entertainment.

"No, son, East Geddie ain't east of Geddie," he'd say cheerfully, proud to own such knowledge. "East Geddie is east of Old Geddie, which is southwest of Geddie itself, of course. You got to go back west, to Geddie, then go south on the Ammon Road, then turn west again on the Old Geddie Road, and keep headin' west till you get to East Geddie."

I used to think that there was a town near where we lived called Geddie Itself, because that's how people usually re-ferred to the town we were supposed to be east of.

I stopped at the welcome station last time I came down here and got a free state road map, and East Geddie is still, cartographically speaking, east of Geddie. I'm sure lots of people driving through on the way to the beach think the place is one of those ghost towns that cease to exist for several decades before anyone notifies the map makers.

Up in the plunder room at Daddy's, there's an old chest of Aunt Connie's, where the family kept deeds and old letters from back as far as the late 1700s. My grandmother, when she was a young woman, tried to get East Geddie's history onto a page of lined paper:

Malcolm Geddie run the Tavern on the old Indian Trail, for them that came from Cool Spring to Port Campbell.

Littlejohn

He come from Scotland. It was called Cole Geddie's,
because they didn't serve meals. They got to calling the
hole area Cole Geddie's. Then it was Cole Geddie. Then
it was Geddie. Then folks come up from the Blue Sandhills
to work at the Sawmill. They bilt east of Geddie, so they
was East Geddie. Then they bilt the Rail Road from Cool
Spring to Port Campbell, but Neil McNeil wouldn't let
them have any of his Land, so they bilt the Rail Road north
of Geddie, and they called the Town at the Rail Road
station Geddie Station. Geddie Station grew, and it
become Geddie. The first Geddie become Old Geddie.
East Geddie stayed East Geddie. They tried to change it,
but my husband, Mr. John McCain, knowed as Red John,
said at the meeting in 1904, We was East Geddie because
we was East of Geddie. We ain't moved. We are still East
Geddie. And so they nevver changed it.

I wish I could get my students to write so economically.
Like Red John McCain, I can be a little intractable. Maybe
that's why I've made such a pig's breakfast of things.

I've been in Europe for half the summer and am still trying
to sort everything out. I didn't leave any addresses or phone
numbers, even though Daddy always wants me to. Even at
eighty-two, he wants to know where I am. Even at forty, I
let it bother me and try to shut him out.

When I called the Carlsons from England to see how
Justin was doing, they told me about his flight to Carolina.
I wasn't a happy camper, but I had a few weeks to cool off.
This hasn't been any easier for Justin than it has for me.

If last year had been a football game, God would have been
called for unnecessary roughness. In April, they discovered

Mom's pancreatic cancer, and by November, she was gone. Also in April, I discovered that I was married to an asshole, a problem that has since been corrected.

Daddy was upset about our breakup, but he was so absorbed with Mom that he hardly had time to concentrate on relatively minor catastrophes. And I spared him the gory details, just told him Jeff had moved out.

Christmas was a bad time all around. Justin didn't want to come down, although he and Daddy had always gotten along rather well, even if they didn't have much in common. He sulked most of the time we were at the farm. He was so rude that I couldn't help thinking, if it had been me at fifteen, someone, probably Mom, would have applied severe corporal punishment. I had to cajole and then threaten him into going in and thanking Daddy for the shirt and baseball bat. Everyone just seemed mired in their own private losses. Disaster doesn't necessarily pull the survivors together. Sometimes, we just seem to be trying to push each other off the life raft.

Every memento of Christmas, every cloying TV commercial, every single "Merry Christmas" seemed to drive the dagger a little deeper. We'd been watching television, mainly to keep the lack of conversation from being so conspicuous, on Christmas Eve, when *It's a Wonderful Life* came on unexpectedly at the end of some second-rate college football bowl game. Now we have the movie in our video library; we used to set aside a night to watch it and *Miracle on 34th Street* back-to-back, when Justin was younger. I remember how Jeff used to get kind of choked up by it and pretend he had something in his eye. But the element of surprise made this familiar paean to savings and loans seem like an unexpected Christmas present. We watched raptly. I didn't even bother to sneak a peek at my watch to see how many more hours we had left in East Geddie.

But at the end, when all of George Bailey's friends are filling the basket with money to keep Potter from sending him to prison, and George is holding his daughter, and "Hark the Herald" comes bursting through, Justin got up and stomped out of the room. He didn't come back for the rest of the evening. No one should be made to endure Christmas within at least one year of a personal catastrophe.

Jeff Bowman and I were married a year after I graduated from UNC–Greensboro, when he was a don't-give-a-damn political science graduate from Carolina with no visible future plans other than to stay out of Vietnam and I was working toward a master's in English. We both liked to raise hell and laugh at the rest of the world. But Jeff had to find something to do for a living, and stock brokerage finally offered itself. Soon, we weren't always on the same side.

We lived together for seventeen years, though, and might have just kept going, me an English professor at Montclair, him a broker with Parks and Sutton, mutually enjoying Justin and, on occasions, each other. Bev Lundquist is what tore it.

Jeff and Bev had an affair not long after we were married, but he'd repented, and I'd had my own affair out of revenge, and we somehow patched things up. Sometimes I think we had Justin just to convince each other that we were a real family.

But when Bobby DeVries told me Bev was now working as a secretary for Parks and Sutton, after her divorce, and that things were not good, I started gathering kindling for the funeral pyre of our marriage. Bobby works with Jeff, and he offered to "comfort" me, telling me I was "too good" for Jeff. "Well, then," I told him, "I must be way too good for you." I was already beginning to plot as I showed Bobby the door.

I am not the worst-looking forty-year-old in the world. I have my mother's dark complexion (and temper), and I spend enough time in aerobics to have, thus far, avoided the "well-preserved" stage. My specialty at Montclair is American writers of the early twentieth century. If you teach as long as I have, you learn to mix and match, to teach Fitzgerald and Hemingway and T. S. Eliot and Faulkner and Dreiser in several different ways to different levels of students, rearranging old subjects with new themes. Most of my classes now are for graduate students, where, in the time-honored tradition, we teach to produce teachers.

It is not unusual for one of my students to take a course in *The Waste Land,* in which one starts with Eliot, then branches out to find wasteland imagery in *The Great Gatsby, The Sun Also Rises* and *Look Homeward, Angel.* The same student might then take a course in the short stories of Fitzgerald and Hemingway, then a course in research methods, using the works of Hemingway, Fitzgerald and Eliot with an emphasis on the critical reception of their work. Throw in an obscure Jean Toomer or Ford Madox Ford and your career is set. In fourteen years as a professor at Montclair, girl and woman, I have never taught a course that did not include at least one work from either Fitzgerald or Hemingway. Once every year or so, I teach a course on feminism in literature. The main text is *Save Me the Waltz* by Zelda Fitzgerald. Of course, it's necessary for my students in this course to read *Tender Is the*

Night in order to do an analysis of the Zelda characters in each book.

At Montclair, we use some of the brightest and most obsequious Ph.D. candidates as poorly paid graduate instructors, mostly to commit *Beowulf* on innocent freshmen. One of the instructors, Maxton Winfree, was a twenty-five-year-old protégé of mine with an unpublished novel and half another one. Max intended to subsidize his creative genius by attaching himself to the financial security of Montclair or someplace similar, allegedly as a teacher. I'd read his novel and felt he said little, badly. But he would serve my purpose well.

No one can teach such romantic stuff as *The Great Gatsby* and *A Farewell to Arms* without being the object of a few schoolboy crushes. I had always been flattered by such attention, especially as the years went by. I was always kind but firm; and if Jeff hadn't resurrected Bev Lundquist, poor Max Winfree would have been let down gently.

Only two weeks before my Great Revelation, Max had made his move. He invited me to his apartment after a faculty meeting, supposedly to get my opinion on a problem he was having with setting in his second novel. (You should set it aside, I was thinking, and get a job.) He fixed us each a bourbon and water, then sat beside me while he described the problem. He slipped his arm behind me on his little student-issue couch as he talked, playing with my hair. Then he moved in, awkwardly, for the kiss. I turned and we bumped heads, causing him to spill half his bourbon. He pledged his unyielding devotion, I gave him my happy-wife-and-mother speech and we parted with a minimum of embarrassment. Since then, we'd spoken several times, once in private as he slipped into my ten-by-ten office, closed the door quickly behind him and told me how much my friendship meant to him.

After I found out what was keeping Jeff from coming home until seven on Tuesday and Friday nights, though, and who accompanied him to Denver for the business trip in October, my thoughts turned to Max.

"I have to see you," I told him over the office phone, speaking to the instrument of my revenge three doors away. "It's very important. . . . No, not here. Come by my house at five-thirty. . . . No, I can't tell you over the phone."

Back in Cotton Hall at UNC–G, other girls in the dorm would beg me to answer the phone as their proxy when prospective blind dates from Chapel Hill called. Looks come and go, but a good voice lasts. When I say, "I have to see you," better than Max Winfree have come running.

It was a Friday in April, a week before we found out about Mom. Justin was spending the night with Trey Carlson, three blocks away. Jeff would be at his Friday after-work poker session, a habit he'd started last summer, shortly before Bev Lundquist started working for him. I wondered, grinding my teeth, if Jeff and his broker buddies got a few laughs out of the double entendre of "poker." At any rate, I would count on him to arrive within five minutes of seven, faithful even in his infidelity. It had been all I could do the previous Friday to restrain myself from dinging him with a Jefferson cup when he came through the door, all fake cheerfulness, so full of guilt I couldn't believe I hadn't sensed it on my own.

At 5:25, Max Winfree's banged-up secondhand Isuzu pulled into the drive. He got out, closing the door carefully so as not to disturb the neighbors, and came up the walk to the front door. I waited until he rang the bell, looking nervously over his shoulder as if the irate husband might come wheeling up at any second.

"Come in, Max," I said, trying to put as much heat into those three little words as possible. I was wearing an old pair of form-fitted jeans and a silk blouse, no bra. I could feel my nipples puckering in the late-afternoon chill. I used to go braless around the house a lot because Jeff liked it, but I had seldom gone public, so to speak.

He closed the door, leaned down and kissed me. I let him, meeting his tongue with mine as he placed his left hand on the small of my back and his right hand a bit lower.

"Wait," I said, moving back a step. "Go outside and move the car out of the driveway. I don't want the neighbors to see."

In his present state, Max didn't bother to dwell for long on how much more suspicious it looked for him to back his car down the drive, park it two doors down on the street and then walk back to our house. He was a bit distracted.

When he returned, he let himself in. I had mixed a couple of black Russians, mine a bit stronger than his, and did my best to restrict things to kissing and a little petting for the time being. Relax, I told him, we've got all night. My son's at a friend's house, and my husband's on a business trip. Monkey-business trip, I thought. On my way home, a little after four, I had detoured through a neighborhood I'd looked up on the city map. There, at 207 Park, was Jeff's burgundy Cressida. I never have liked to leave anything to chance.

Finally, at twenty minutes to seven, after two black Russians, a lot of kissing and a fair amount of fondling, mostly by Max, I stood up, unbuttoned my silk blouse and took it off. I felt a little foolish, but black Russians are great at drowning inhibitions. Max started forward, but I motioned for him to wait. He started to take his shirt off, but I told him, "I want to do that myself."

I laid the blouse on the floor, then took off my sandals, setting them down in a straight line between the couch and the master bedroom door. Next came the jeans and then, at heaven's gate itself, my panties. I led Max inside and told him to wait. I guess he never bothered to wonder why I would be concerned enough to remove two drink glasses from the coffee table and put them in the kitchen.

When I got back to the bedroom, I locked the door from the inside. Max was already down to his shorts and was out of them in about two seconds. Not bad, I thought, and realized maybe I was enjoying this a little more than I'd planned. Oh well, you can't plan everything. I led him over to our brass queen-size bed, where he planted his tongue solidly in my ear and started stroking my thigh, higher, higher . . .

"Wait," I said, rolling away just before we went over the edge. I stood up and went to the dresser, opened the bottom drawer and pulled out the ropes.

"Indulge an old lady," I told him, stretching the two elastic cords back and forth like an accordion, trying to look like I did this all the time. I hit on this part of the plan the day I had to haul the lawnmower to the repair shop in the trunk of the car. Jeff had bought this elastic rope with hooks on each end to tie down the trunk lid when something was too large to fit with it closed. I bought another one just like it at the hardware store on the way home.

I pushed Max back on the bed and crawled on top of him. I wrapped the first cord around his left wrist, hooking that end to one of the vertical brass posts at the head of the bed, then wrapped the other end around his right wrist and attached the hook to the bed on that side.

"Boy, you older women are kinda kinky," Max said, trying to inject a note of levity. I could see that he was a little taken aback at the thought of a woman seizing complete control. If he noticed the white rectangle on the sliding glass door that led out to the deck, or if he wondered why someone fastidious enough to clean up drink glasses wouldn't bother to close the blinds before screwing one of her graduate students, he kept it to himself.

I tied his feet the same way, leaving him spread-eagled on the bed. I sneaked a peak at my digital watch, my only item of clothing: 6:54. I turned on the lamp light, explaining, "I like to watch," then mounted him. Just like that. Fifteen years of fidelity out the window.

I was trying to keep control of myself and Max, and I wondered if this would be the one night that Jeff was both unfaithful and late. Then, after what seemed like a very long time, with the watch showing 7:02 and Max writhing and groaning underneath me, I heard the Cressida pull into the driveway.

"Oh shit," said Max, noticeably shrinking from the task.

"Listen," I said, shushing him, "if you remain quiet, and don't panic, everything will be all right. You really don't have much choice anyhow, do you?" and I gave him a reassuring smile as I wriggled a little bit to regain his full attention.

I could hear the car door close, then heard Jeff fumble

with the keys and, finally, open the front door. Our house is a contemporary, with a large living room, where Max and I had been, under a cathedral ceiling. The master bedroom is back and to the right, past the kitchen. I could imagine Jeff following the trail of clothes to the bedroom door, where my panties were hanging on the doorknob with a note pinned to them: USE THE OTHER DOOR.

Jeff knows I like to play games. One Halloween, after he'd gotten up about a dozen times to take care of trick-or-treaters at the door while I worked on a research paper, I had slipped out of my clothes, into a raincoat and out the side door. I rang the front bell, and when he answered, I flung the coat open and said, "Trick or treat!" It was this, my willingness to go the extra mile, to give 110 percent, that really pissed me off when I found out about Bev Lundquist. I mean, what did he want?

I figured Jeff was feeling a little guilty right now, was depending on that, in fact. He would go back to the kitchen, then through the door to the porch, which led to the deck, which led to the sliding-glass door I was looking out from atop Max Winfree. Maybe Jeff wouldn't want to be amorous tonight. Maybe he couldn't be amorous anymore tonight, I thought, grinding my teeth and grinding Max a little, too.

I could hear Jeff at the bedroom door, then listened as he walked back to the kitchen, moving, I thought, a little hesitantly. I saw him come out on the screen porch, then go through the door to the deck. He was about halfway across when he probably realized that having to satisfy two women in one night was not his biggest problem.

Through the sliding-glass door that I had secured with the

charley bar from inside, I saw Jeff go from sheepish to shocked as we stared at each other through the triple-pane glass. I worked up the most devastating sneer I could manage under, or rather over, the circumstances, slowly raised my right hand in his direction and offered him my middle finger.

A husband with a clear conscience probably would have broken the glass door or gone back inside and kicked in the main bedroom door with my panties still hanging on it. But Jeff Bowman's conscience was about as muddy as a mountain creek after a spring flood. If he needed any further evidence of my primary motive, he needed to look no farther than the cardboard message taped to the sliding-glass door, the one I'd written with a red Magic Marker just before Max arrived. It said: GO BACK TO 207 PARK, ASSHOLE. And so he did.

He left quietly, and I eventually untied Max, with whom I slept two more times out of gratitude. But I didn't want to be around when Max finally realized that a lack of talent would doom him to teaching others how to write.

I left the door open for Jeff, leaving it for him to decide whether I sought freedom or just revenge. I wasn't sure myself. We're both strong-willed people, and neither of us ever apologized for much. He just came over during the day one Thursday and took away most of his clothes. It was almost a month before we spoke, and by then I think we both realized that any life we shared would be of a considerably diminished nature, accusations and despair no farther away than one wrong word.

He still lives with Bev Lundquist, with no apparent plans to marry, and I've spent the shank of the summer traveling around Europe with Mark Hammaker. Mark's forty-eight, he's managing editor of the daily paper here, the *Montclair Light,* and we've had some good times. We might have some more. I don't know.

Justin stayed with Jeff and Bev as much as he wanted after we broke up. The reason Justin had to turn to his grandfather for help, I guess, is that I didn't want him with Mark and me in Europe, and Jeff and Bev didn't want him with them at Hilton Head, where they spent most of June and July. I told him there was no way we could afford for him to go to Europe, too. He didn't take it well. I thought he'd get over his hurt spending the summer with Trey and the Carlsons.

We had to sell our contemporary with the deck and porch after the separation and divorce, and Justin and I moved into a town house near the university and Justin's high school. Justin seemed to take it all in stride, just grew quieter and taller. I never slept over at Mark's unless Justin was staying with friends.

The past school year, though, Justin's grades started to slip. Most upsetting to me, he was doing poorly in English. This boy, who was read to from good books as soon as he could listen, who read *Robinson Crusoe* at eight and *The Catcher in the Rye* at twelve, almost flunked sophomore English, after nothing but A's and B's all through elementary and junior high school.

He doesn't like Mark much, which hardly surprises me. Mark is a disciplinarian. When his own son got a little wild his senior year in high school, Mark sent him to Fork Union, a military school, to "straighten him out." He'd like to do the same with Justin. Over my dead body. Mark's son now lives in San Francisco and visits him every two years or so.

Justin seems to take a perverse delight in rejecting everything I've ever tried to teach him. Anything I think is trash, Justin immediately adopts. Pulp science fiction, rap music, sit-coms for the brain-damaged. His group at school seems to consist mainly of other professors' sons and daughters, most of them suffering from an imbalance of love and knowledge.

CHAPTER FOUR

August 8

It was early June when I looked up from my hoeing and saw a ghost coming toward me.

Ever since Sara died, I had took care of the flower beds she used to love, and that morning I was hoeing away, thinking about Lafe, about how you could spy him half a mile away, walking in from the fields or from hunting, with that red hair of his that looked so much like Daddy's in the old pictures. I always looked more like Momma, who was a Geddie.

The ghost was maybe a hundred yards away, which is about all the far I can see anymore. It was walking kind of tired, like it was climbing uphill. It had a sack on its back, throwed over its shoulder and held with one hand, the other arm swinging free to help it get through the sand in the old rut road. Lafe had surely come back, was surely coming home with some Irish potatoes he'd dug out of the hill for Momma.

"Looks like you got enough taters there to last us all winter," I said to Lafe's ghost. By now, it was close enough, maybe fifty feet away, for me to see that the hair was different. It was short, like Lafe's, but it was spikier, rougher looking.

"What in the world have you done to your hair?" I asked the ghost, leaning on the hoe handle to keep from falling.

The ghost stopped five feet from me and said, "Grand-daddy, are you all right?"

It was Justin, my grandson.

He set down this bag, the one I'd thought was full of potatoes, and said he'd come to visit me. He looked like he'd been rode hard and hung up wet. I reckon I took a little while to shift gears and get my poor addled brain back to the real world. Finally I asked him what in the world he was doing in East Geddie, and where his momma was, and then I remembered that she was in Europe somewhere.

Justin reached out to shake my hand. He's near-bout grown, must be at least six foot two, but he don't weigh more than 150 pounds. Him and me never seemed like we

had all that much in common, and it struck me as queer that
he was telling me he'd just decided to come down for a visit,
with Georgia in Europe and all. But he appeared to need
some looking after.

"I reckon we better get you something to eat," I told
him. "You look about half starved. Come on in the house."

I took some biscuits out of the freezer, wrapped them in
tinfoil and put them in the toaster oven, then got some ham
out of the refrigerator and started frying it in the skillet. We
had three more jars of Sara's peach preserves left, so I got
some of them down, then got some apple jelly. I hadn't done
much entertaining here lately, so I was just reaching for
anything that might of been good to eat. Lord, I don't know
what-all they eat up in Virginia.

I found some cold fried chicken left over from some Jenny
had brought me. I offered to warm up some collards, knowing Justin thinks about as much of them as I do, just to try
and get him to smile.

We set down at the big old dining-room table where eight
of us used to eat three meals a day, and Justin started to spear
a couple of pieces of ham with his fork. I reckon he noticed
that I hadn't moved yet, and he remembered where he was.

"Would you like to ask the blessing, Justin?" I asked him.

"No thank you, Granddaddy," he said.

I bowed my head.

"Kind heavenly father, bless this meal we are about to
partake of, and bless our loved ones here and abroad, that
they may come back to us safely. Amen."

I opened my eyes and saw Justin staring from across the
table.

"Well, go ahead," I told him. "It's blessed. Dig in."

Littlejohn

. . .

Daddy's name was John, and everybody called him Red John. He lost a leg somewhere in Virginia, maybe in the Wilderness Campaign. By the time he married Momma, he was forty-nine years old. Momma's name was Faith Geddie, and she was Daddy's third cousin's daughter, which wasn't considered peculiar at that time. What was unusual was that she was just twenty-three and had already lost one husband, to the flu, three years earlier. They say that when her husband died, his folks sent her back with six hogs and twenty dollars. So I reckon she was happy to accept Red John McCain's offer.

Lex and Connie was born first. Daddy, who got to choose all the first names, named them Lexington and Concord, which was funny names, even for around here. You couldn't hardly tell that they was twins. Since they was boy and girl, they weren't hardly identical. The year after, they had another boy, John Geddie McCain after my daddy. He died when he was three weeks old. Gruff was born in 1898. His real name is Cerrogordo, after a battle in the Mexican War. Lord knows what possessed Daddy to name him that. They say he got his nickname because he had a pouty look to him all the time, and one time an old aunt said, "What a gruff young un you are!" and it stuck, the way things like that will. I think anybody named Cerrogordo would be glad to be named Gruff.

Because Century was born in 1900, that was her name. Another baby, a girl, was born dead the next year. Then, in 1903, Momma had Lafe. Daddy named him after the Marquis de Lafayette. Marquis de Lafayette McCain. He was real happy to be called Lafe.

I come last. They said Daddy wanted to name me John Geddie McCain, but Momma wouldn't let him, since it would insult the memory of her dead baby. Up to this point, she was in charge of middle names, and maybe to offset some of Daddy's foolishness, she give every one of her children the same middle name: Geddie.

"Besides," she's supposed to of told Daddy, "how are you going to explain to this baby how come there's a tombstone out there in the graveyard with his name on it?"

Daddy thought about it for a spell, and they say I didn't have any name a-tall for several days. Finally, Daddy told the rest of the children that he had the perfect name. Considering his record to this point, I'm sure Momma was uneasy.

"We'll call him Littlejohn," he told Momma and them.

They said Momma only asked him one question: "One word or two?"

I reckon after Lexington, Concord, Cerrogordo, Century and Marquis de Lafayette, she didn't think Littlejohn Geddie McCain was all that bad a name.

Aunt Mallie delivered me. She was ninety-seven years old, and she had delivered Daddy, too. She was living in the same old slave cabin her husband, Zebediah, and Captain McCain, who was my granddaddy, built over sixty years before, right after the captain married into the Geddies and got his land and slaves. She lived to be 104. Two days after her funeral, Daddy and them went down to the cabin, and all her family, nieces and nephews and what-all, had left. They never come back.

Aunt Mallie read fortunes. Momma didn't hold to such foolishness, but all us young-uns sneaked away at one time or another to have Aunt Mallie look at our palms and tell our futures. Century and Lafe sneaked me down to her place one day when I was five, so I reckon she was 102 years old.

She still dipped snuff, and I can remember the whole cabin smelling like it. She took my palm in her big old wrinkled hand and studied it real hard. She shook her head while Century and Lafe giggled behind her. She was about deaf, so I don't reckon she minded. I never forgot what she told me.

"You got a hard road, boy," she said. She spoke so low I couldn't hardly hear her. "I see real bad times, but then I see a whole lot of happy times. Don't be giving up on the good times. They be coming. The Lord Jesus is got some surprises in store for you, to be sure."

I don't reckon anybody ever give Aunt Mallie enough credit.

CHAPTER FIVE

June 27

Granddaddy is praying. I can hear him right through the wall between his room and mine. I can't tell what he's saying, but the sound of his voice wakes me up every morning at 7:30. If I ever live to be that old, I'm going to sleep until noon every day.

I've been here three weeks now, and this part never changes. Next, he'll go to the bathroom, wash and shave, then he'll start fixing breakfast. He sings while he cooks, and he cooks the same thing every day, almost. There's fried sausage and scrambled eggs, along with the biscuits he takes out of the freezer for us every night and heats up in the oven the next morning. We have apple jelly and peach preserves—or we did until we ran out this week—and milk. For some reason, Granddaddy puts ice in his milk, and it forms a little skim at the top. I've finally gotten him to serve me mine without ice.

He and I clean up the dishes. I watched him wash them the first two mornings I was here, and then he handed me a cloth and said, "Here. Time you earned your keep."

He finishes getting dressed, then goes out on the back porch, where the overhang keeps out the morning sun, and he reads the local paper. It's called the *Port Campbell Post,* and it has about the worst sports pages I've ever seen. Nothing about anything out of North Carolina except for the major-league baseball box scores and a couple of paragraphs on every game, and they don't even have the West Coast night games. But he reads every word. He's a Minnesota Twins fan, because the Twins used to play in Washington, something I didn't know, although Dad might have told me once. Granddaddy reads all the world news, commenting on an earthquake in Bolivia or the Russians in Afghanistan, and then he turns to the obituaries.

"Oh, Lord," he'll say, "Abel Bullard's dead," like I might ever have known or cared to know Abel Bullard. And then he'll explain to me that Abel Bullard, on the outside chance I didn't instantly know, was the brother of Miss Hattie Bullard, who used to sing in the choir at church, about a thousand years before I was born.

Granddaddy isn't completely out of it, though, not by a long shot. It took him about three days to see through that scam I cooked up about wanting to come visit him. I guess he knew the number of times I previously had wanted to come visit him amounted to approximately zero.

It turns out that the Carlsons went apeshit when they found out I had run away. They called all over town, even had the police looking for me. Mom, naturally, hadn't told them where Granddaddy lived, and all Trey knew was that we had relatives somewhere in North Carolina. Also, Mom, the scatterbrain, didn't bother to tell them where Dad and the lovely Beverly were staying. Trey knew they were going to South Carolina, somewhere. I was counting on Trey's failure to comprehend geography. But I guess his parents would have been a little embarrassed to tell Mom that her pride and joy had been misplaced. Not that she'd care. Also, she didn't give them any addresses in Europe. She didn't give me any, either.

But Granddaddy had insisted, unknown to me, that Mom give him the Carlsons' address and phone number. He always wants her to tell him everywhere she's staying when she travels, but she never does, and it pisses her off that he keeps asking.

Anyhow, he calls the Carlsons after he sends me to the store for groceries, and they tell him what's been going on. By this time, the store detective and the Montclair school system have filled them in on all the gory details, and they, of course, tell Granddaddy everything. He tells me the jig's up, an old expression of his, when I get back, and says he'll give me one minute to come clean or he's sending me back to Virginia on the first bus out.

Littlejohn

· · ·

It all started when Mom told me she was going to Europe
and that I could stay with the Carlsons, like this was some
kind of great favor she was bestowing on me. You didn't
even like Europe the last time we took you, she said when
I pitched a bitch. That was three years ago, I said. I was a
child. You were happy enough to stay with friends the last
two times we went, she said, and then she went on about
how I was trying to mess things up between her and Mark
the Narc. I call him that because Mom never found the dope
I keep hid in my room until she started dating him, and I'm
sure he put her up to looking. Hell, he might have even
searched my room himself, in which case I would never
forgive Mom for letting him. Mark the Narc wants me in
Fork Union, wearing a smart little uniform and standing at
attention, so bad he can taste it. Then he can move in. I tell
Mom this, and that she can go to China with him if she wants,
just forget about me, and she accuses me of laying a guilt trip
on her. We didn't talk much the last two weeks before she
left.

The day of finals in English, I skipped. I meant to go, and
I had studied about twenty minutes, which is massive for me,
the night before, because I was very close to flunking and
facing the heartbreak of summer school. Mom acted like
they'd take her job away or something if I flunked English,
like if she was a minister and they found out her son was a
Satan worshipper or something.

I went to school that day, or got as far as the parking lot,
at least. It's only a six-block walk, one of the reasons Mom
moved to the town house after she and Dad split, she's
always reminding me, like this is a great sacrifice or some-

43

thing. But as I walked through the parking lot, here come Tony Linhart and Kyle Waters in Tony's new red Sunbird his dad bought for him; bastard's so rich there ought to be a law. And they've both passed out of exams, so they have the day off.

"Goin' up to Washpon," Kyle says. "Want to come along?"

I guess I'm easily led. Washpon is this lake at the bottom of the Blue Ridge, where everybody from Montclair goes to party. I got in, and English was history.

I forged the grade to a D and got Mom to sign the report card just before she left, and I swear I had every intention of signing up for summer school and having the whole thing straightened out by the time Mom got back.

But then Marcia and I went over to the university two days after Mom left to find this guy we hoped would sell us an ounce. He works in the campus bookstore, and I wanted to find out when he'd be home, so I could come around. While I was waiting for him to take care of a couple of customers, I saw this pair of shades on the rack about halfway down the aisle that I really needed. We'd been doing a little lifting here and there, and it had gotten so it almost seemed like they must know we were doing it, we were so obvious. So, I slipped these shades off their little holder and into the big pocket of my Army surplus jacket. Marcia was standing next to me. She's a fox, blond page-boy cut, bedroom eyes, body that won't quit, real tough for fourteen. All of a sudden, there's this old guy I've never seen before, short hair and a white shirt with sweat stains under both arms, clip-on tie, a real dork, and he's saying, like, come with me, please, except he doesn't say please the way somebody does when they're asking. The way he says it, "please" translates as "or I'll break your arm."

He also hustles Marcia along, and she's cussing the guy, telling him to get his goddamn hands off her. He takes us into a room at the back of the store, and there's this closed-circuit TV where he can see the whole store. He just sits there all day, I guess. Like maybe he gets a bounty for every desperado he brings in.

I've got to tell you, I kind of lose it. I beg him not to arrest me, tell him my mom is at Sloan-Kettering in New York being treated for cancer. Marcia cuts me a look, like, what the hell is Sloan-Kettering and where did you dig that one up? He makes us both sweat, insists that Marcia is in on it, too, for about thirty minutes. Then he tells us he's going to give us a break, but somehow, looking at this guy, I don't think this is going to be quite as good as winning the lottery. He won't have us arrested, he says, but he insists that we both bring our parents in so he can talk with them about our little crime spree. I tell him, again, that my mom isn't home, and that my dad is out of the state. Who am I staying with? he asks. When I tell him, he tells me I'll have to bring the Carlsons in. He has our names and addresses by this time, and he's checked the phone book to make sure we're not shucking him, so we're caught.

I really feel bad for Marcia, because she's got to face both parents and deal with this right now, and her folks are so tight they squeak. They will ground her until she graduates and forbid her to see me until she's like fifty. I also feel bad because I've begged and whimpered in front of my girl, in addition to getting her into more trouble than she thinks she can handle right now. I also am not looking forward to telling the Carlsons that their house guest for the next six weeks is an apprehended if not convicted shoplifter. Christ, at that point they didn't even know they had to help me register for summer school because I didn't really pass English.

So, faced with a future of being straightened out at Fork Union after being ostracized by polite society and, much worse, Marcia and all her living relatives, I split. I went home that same Thursday afternoon, packed everything I thought I could carry in my backpack, took most of the money out of my account that Mom left there for my summer fun, wrote the Carlsons this spaced-out note about taking a little time to get my head together and left. Trey had been at a job interview or he'd have been in it as deep as Marcia and me.

I'm dumb, but I'm not terminally stupid. There have been kids from here who went to New York and were never seen again. I just wanted to get away, not commit suicide. I wasn't sure about the best way to thumb to Granddaddy's, but he was the only one who came to mind for some reason, the only one I thought might take me in, no questions asked. I figured he'd be so out of it, he wouldn't mind.

I bought a road map at the Exxon station and sat down on the corner to read it. Route 35 would take me south almost to the state line, it looked like, and from there I'd have to take a bunch of dippy little state roads to get to East Geddie. But it was cheaper than taking the bus, and there wasn't one going that way from Montclair for five hours, the guy at the station said. By then, they'd have my picture on the post-office wall.

So, I walked the mile down to the bypass and stuck out my thumb. It went real well for a while. Two coeds going down to Sweet Briar picked me up and got me almost all the way to Lynchburg. Then a construction worker in a pickup, not as friendly as the college girls, but a ride nevertheless, drove me all the way past Danville.

By this time, it was getting late, about seven, I guess, and I must have stood there, watching rednecks in white T-shirts drive by giving me the fish eye for like an hour and a half before this bubba stops, asks me where I'm going. I tell him East Geddie, North Carolina. It obviously does not compute. I mean, this guy's probably never been out of the county. It's a wonder they let him out of the house.

"Don't know that one," he says, "but I'm goin' down to Zion Springs."

I don't know Zion Springs from bedsprings, but anything beats standing, so I get in this car you have to open from the inside. We go about twelve miles, just far enough to be away from everything, when he puts on his turn signal, and I see the sign, ZION SPRINGS 8, pointing to the left. I ask him to let me out there, and he gives me this snaggle-toothed grin as I get out, 'cause he knows there's no way in hell anybody else is going to pick me up out here, especially now that it's almost dark.

I stand there for two hours. I've thumbed a lot around Montclair, and there's a theory I've got about it. You have to believe you're going to get a ride in order for a car to stop. If you believe you're not going to get a ride, that you don't deserve a ride, that you're not worthy to ride in that fine Buick coming toward you, the driver gets the message sure as hell. When you get to that point, you might as well start walking.

The trouble was, I was still more than a hundred miles from Port Campbell, which is like another six from East

Geddie, the best I could add up the little numbers between towns on the map. And the next town south of where I was standing was nine miles away.

So I'm standing there, walking awhile, thumbing awhile, and it's like eleven o'clock. I get to this white-trash store that's just closed, but there's a Coke machine outside, and somebody has thrown an apple, with only one bite out of it, in the trash can. It's just sitting there on top. I must be pretty hungry, because I take it out, try to pull the skin and meat away from the part that's been bitten and eat it. That's supper, and breakfast looks like it might be a long way down the road. I'm kicking myself for not having the construction worker just let me out at a McDonald's we passed back in Danville. I can taste a Big Mac.

There's not much left to do but climb the twenty-foot embankment on the side of the road and try to sleep. Even in June, it gets cold as a bitch outside late at night. I put the backpack down for a pillow, take out another shirt and put it over my shoulders, roll a joint and smoke it all. It probably takes me like ten seconds to fall asleep, I'm so wasted.

I dream we're at the big Fourth of July celebration they have at Michie Park back home, the one we used to go to when I was a little kid. All the fireworks are going off up above us, and I'm sitting between Mom and Dad, who are sitting close enough together that I can feel and smell both of them. I'm kind of scared, and Dad looks down at me and smiles and says something, but I can't hear him because of all the noise.

And, of course, the way things have been going lately, I wake up in the middle of *Bambi, Part II*. You know, the one where six raving rednecks freeze a deer with their truck's headlights alongside a deserted highway at three in the morning, then get out and calmly blast him to Swiss cheese. There aren't any houses around, but these guys act a little nervous, anyhow, and I hope they don't see me. Winding up as a road kill is not my life's burning ambition. They drag the deer over to the truck and manage to lift and push him into the back. Before they roar off, I can see the dark spot on the side of the road, staining the white line, where the deer fell. Then they're gone, and I'm wide awake, shaking like a bitch, partly from the cold. I wish I was back in Montclair, hassles and all, and I damn near decide to turn my ass around and start thumbing north, although I know by now that it would not be smart to stand alongside this road after dark, at least not without a sign that says NOT A DEER.

About two years later, the sun finally comes up. It's beautiful from my spot up over the road, but I realize I must have picked the coldest place for miles, because I'm on top of an exposed hill where I can see east for just about ever. I stumble down the embankment, feeling froggy as hell and sore and tired and very, very hungry. In less than five minutes, before I wake up and realize I don't deserve a ride, an old man, looks almost as old as Granddaddy, stops and takes me all the way to Durham, lets me out right in front of a Burger King. I order a couple of those croissant things, along with a large Pepsi. The croissants make me think of Mom, because on the last trip the three of us took to Paris, she must have spent fifteen minutes with me one morning at our hotel teaching me how to pronounce it, so I could order breakfast for all of us. What I want to know is, why do the French put all those letters in their words if they're not going to say them?

It takes me until almost lunch to get to Granddaddy's. One guy is going as far as Benson, another one takes me to Port Campbell, right to Highway 47, and then another one drops me off at a place called the Hit 'n' Run, right in Geddie. From there, I walk to his house.

He looks older than I remember him, but maybe I just haven't been paying much attention. I'm already thinking, damn, he needs help worse than I do. He's obviously got me mixed up for somebody else at first, and when we go inside, I see he's got notes on everything. There's a note telling him to turn off the oven, except he's spelled it "trun"—Mom said he's had trouble spelling all his life—one telling him how to warm stuff in the microwave, instructions on the washer-dryer on how, step by step, to do the clothes. These seem to be in Grandma's handwriting, and the paper is kind of yellowed.

But he has his own way of doing things, and as long as nothing gets in the way of his routine, he's usually all right. Guess that makes me a welcome addition. He gets my name wrong like about half the time, usually calls me Lafe, which was one of his brothers' name, the one that got killed in a hunting accident, I think. Sometimes, he'll start off with Lafe, then go to Mom, before he finally gets to me, like "Lafe . . . I mean, Georgia . . . I mean, Justin!" After I'd been here two weeks, and he'd done that about a million times, I went to my room, got a sheet of notebook paper out, wrote JUSTIN on it in big red letters and taped it to my forehead. When I came back in the dining room, which is also where the TV is and where visitors sit in cold weather, he looked at me, kind of surprised, with his mouth open a little more than it normally is. Then he said, "Son, if you ever live to be as old as me, you'll be happy if you can just remember your own name.''

He's probably right. I mean, like I can't believe his father fought in the Civil War. Trey's great-great-great-grandfather fought in it, and I had to borrow Mom's copy of this ''history'' that my great-grandmother wrote before Trey would believe it.

Actually, my great-grandfather and great-great-grandfather both fought in the Civil War. My great-great-grandfather was called Captain McCain, but the history said he wasn't a real captain in anybody's army until the Civil War, when they let him lead the home guard, which I guess was like the geezers and kids and crips. He was supposed to have led these jokers up to the federal arsenal in Port Campbell and demanded that the Union troops surrender, even though he had just a few old guys with hunting guns with him. According to the history, the lieutenant asked him, ''Is that all the men you have brought to take my arsenal?'' And my great-great-grandfather was supposed to have said, ''The woods is full of them. The Geddie boys is everywhere.'' And they surrendered! Of course, my mom said the guys in the arsenal were probably Southerners anyhow and couldn't wait to surrender and join the other side.

My great-grandfather, who was called Red John, had lost his leg in the real fighting. He came home and was in the home guard, too. They had this battle, right down in Old Geddie, where the black people live now, when Captain McCain and Red John and a bunch of other dumb shits tried to attack some Union army troops that were doing a little raping and pillaging on their way north. The history said a bunch of the home guard got killed, and the rest escaped over into the Blue Sandhills, where they apparently hid until the Yankees finished burning down everything they could find, including the captain's house. Smart move, guys.

Anyway, Granddaddy gets in touch with the Carlsons, and then I come clean with him, except about the dope, because I don't think Granddaddy can handle that, and he might search my things. But I tell him I flunked English, which is not a flash to him, since the Carlsons already told him, and my girlfriend will never be allowed to speak to me again, and my mom is going to marry a guy who'll send me to military school for the rest of my life, and she doesn't care anything about me, anyhow.

He takes it all except the last part. He gets a little red in the face and starts reading me the riot act about how "ugly" I'm acting toward my mother, and about how hard it's been for her, getting divorced and all, and about how most children—I guess he's so old he still thinks of me as a child—would be happy to have a mother so smart and pretty.

I get mad, too, and go to my room to start packing things, actually just throwing them into the backpack. I'm doing such a piss-poor job of it that half the stuff won't fit. I storm out the front door like I know where I'm going, a couple of shirts and some underwear still back on the bed. The screen door makes that singing sound it always makes when somebody slams it hard. Granddaddy calls after me, but I've got to get out of there. I can get a job somewhere, sleep at the Y, whatever.

I'm already on the paved road, headed back into East Geddie, when he pulls up alongside me in the pickup.

"Come on and get in the truck, son," he says. I keep walking. He keeps moving the truck up in jerks and starts, trying to talk to me. We must go down the road a couple of hundred yards like this. Two cars go by, and now we're beside this mobile home, and some gap-toothed old hag is sitting on the little wooden steps in front, staring at us.

I finally get back in to keep him from getting rear-ended by some of the maniacs around here. We go to the little store in the middle of town, and we sit in the truck and talk.

"The folks that are keeping you said you could stay here if you want to," he tells me. "I told them I could get you all straightened out about summer school. And they already talked to the man you stole the sunglasses from."

I'm crying by now. He goes in the store and comes back out with a couple of Cokes, and we sit there in the shade and talk. He tells me how proud he's always been of me, and I wonder how anybody could be proud of me right now. He tells me how much I remind him of his brother Lafe, who he says was the good-looking one, and the smart one, in the family. Some family, I'm thinking. He says that he's never forgotten how I could read when I was five, and he tells me the story, for the first time since I've been old enough to understand it, about how he didn't learn to read until he was like forty years old. He says he still has the story I wrote for him when I was nine, about the little boy who saves his father's farm by planting magic seeds given to him by an elf that blossom into full-grown pizzas in just three days. Pretty heavy stuff.

He tells me this is as far as he can go, because he's not supposed to drive his truck any farther than the store and the church down the road. He probably shouldn't be driving that far, I'm thinking. He tells me that he has a friend who's a teacher at the local high school, and he might be able to help me get into summer school down here and maybe get that much back in Mom's good graces before she comes home. He's already called the guy, and summer school classes began like today, so I wouldn't miss by starting tomorrow. If I want to, he says.

Well, there isn't much choice, short of just chucking it and starting my lucrative career as a street person. I am not so sure this is going to work out, but at least maybe I'll meet some good-looking fox to take my mind off Marcia, who I only think of every five minutes. Granddaddy says this guy will even give me a ride every morning, good news since that august institution of learning, Sandy Heath High School, is, as Granddaddy says, a right good ways from here.

Next morning, we go through the usual routine. Granddaddy asks me don't I want to dress up a little more the first day, and I point out that my good suit wouldn't fit in the backpack. He kind of chuckles at that. I think maybe he's getting used to the fact that his only grandchild is a wiseass. He says maybe he can get Jenny, my second cousin who's older than Mom, or Harold, her husband, to take me into town, to Belk's or somewhere, to get some clothes. He says he'll pay for them, which is fine by me.

I see this car come tearing down the road, some low, mean machine from the 1960s, it looks like, but in real good shape for something that old.

"That'd be Kenny," Granddaddy says. He's already told me a little about this guy. His name is John Kennedy Locklear, after the old president Mom and Dad think was so great. He seemed like a neat guy—JFK, I mean—but if I see one more television documentary on how the world might just as well have crawled up its own asshole and died after his assassination, I might puke.

This guy, who goes by Kenny but is Mr. Locklear to me, teaches agriculture at the high school, and Granddaddy lets him farm several rows out back of what Granddaddy calls the carhouse, because the guy like lives in a mobile home and doesn't have any land of his own. Granddaddy says Kenny's family used to work for the McCains and lived in the shack down at the edge of the woods. He says Kenny gives him vegetables from what he grows, and that he has gotten more out of the land than any of the McCains ever did. He was in the Army for three years and went two years to N.C. State to study soil science, which doesn't quite sound like nuclear physics, and he's trying to get his degree one course at a time at the local college. He doesn't teach agriculture in the summer, though. How the hell could you fail agriculture? He's a driver's ed teacher in summer school. Good. Maybe I can somehow manage to get a driver's license. I'm sixteen in August, but it'll be fall semester before I can take the classes in Montclair. I'm a little leery, though, of a guy who teaches ag but doesn't own any land and who teaches driver's ed but has a car that's older than he is.

Granddaddy walks out with me, being careful to step across the rusty pipe sticking out of the ground that carries the sink water down to the grease trap by the chicken yard. He has to think about every step, it seems like. He speaks to Kenny, who doesn't get out or cut the engine, and I walk around to the other side to get in. The car's a beauty, must be about twenty-five years old, I guess, and I'm not too far off. He tells me it's a 1965 Impala. It's like white with a red stripe, new red upholstery on the inside, neat as a pin.

"Your granddaddy is a good old man," he says to me as we're heading back out the rut road.

"He speaks well of you," I say, not sure how this guy and I are going to get along. He's a funny-looking dude. He's got this dark skin, but he's not black. Mom said the people who worked as sharecroppers for her family were Lumbees, some kind of Indians. Whatever that is, Kenny must be one. His hair is kind of curly and cut real short. He's wearing a blue shirt and tie, but the shirt's short-sleeve, and I can see the tip of a snake that's tattooed below his right shoulder. He's got some hillbilly music on the radio, and there's a pack of Lucky Strikes on the dash, less the one he's smoking like they're about to repeal them.

We don't talk much. When we get to the high school, I see that someone has stolen the last "h" off Sandy Heath so that the name is Sandy Heat High School. Seems more appropriate. Kenny takes me to the principal's office, where I give them the general details, my version, of how I came to be taking summer school English in Geddie, North Carolina. They tell me they'll have to have my records from Montclair, which I promise I'll have sent, but they're willing to let me start the English course since Granddaddy is my guardian for the summer. Things seem to be a little looser down here. I just hope I can get somebody to send my records.

I've got my textbook, which is more like the one I had in the ninth grade in Montclair. And, praise Jesus, we are going to have *Lord Jim* for required reading. Piece of cake. I read it two years ago.

My classmates, though, are something else. There are eighteen of us in the class, and fifteen of the others are black.

Littlejohn

Three of them are named Geddie. I try to start a conversation with the guy right across from me, guy named Winfrey Geddie who's blacker than the black people ever get up where we live. I tell him I'm from Virginia and he says, "I'm from Old Geddie," which, apparently, passes for high humor around here. I told him my great-grandmother's name was Geddie. "Maybe you and me is related, then," he says, smiling out of one corner of his mouth. "Maybe I'm the black sheep of the family."

I want to tell him I'm not used to living places where all the white people used to own all the black people, but somehow I sense that this would not be appropriate. He does a low five with one of the other Geddies sitting in front of him, and I shut up.

The class itself is a bad joke. Most of these kids apparently have just landed here from Pluto and are being exposed to English for the first time. Mrs. Sessoms, who must be like a year out of college, is basically happy if nobody walks out in the middle of class or calls her "white bitch" during the day. Already now, three weeks into it, I know that this baby is fail-proof. There are kids in Montclair who have failed grades without being real dumb. Down here, they seemed determined to pass everyone, at least until they quit school.

Kenny turns out to be okay, though. He said he went into the Army because his father was killed in Vietnam, but after he got in, he knew that three years would be enough. He said he decided to go to State on the GI bill and become a farmer because that was like all his family had ever done. He also said it was too bad that there wasn't anything there to farm by the time he decided that was what he wanted to do, but that he was saving his money to buy some land. It's a trip to walk with him on the little plot Granddaddy lets him farm. He's only got four rows, about a hundred feet long each, but he's got corn and tomatoes and okra and squash and about four kinds of beans, and cantaloupes and watermelons. He has some peanuts planted that he says won't be ready to pull up until fall, and there are all kinds of greens, too.

He has a metal detector, and sometimes he goes down to where the old shack is and walks around with it, trying to find things. I went down there with him one day, and he came up with a couple of old coins and some kind of metal cup.

One afternoon, he brings me home and, after we have some iced tea, the three of us get in his car and go down past the shack into what they call the swamp. Kenny turns left on a trail beside this big ditch until we get to the family cemetery, a cheerful spot. Granddaddy and Mom and I would come out here sometimes, although Mom never seemed to care much about it; it's been like five years at least since I've seen this part of the farm. Over on the other side of the ditch, we can see people picking their own blueberries, with their cars parked off in the distance. That's Granddaddy's berry farm, which Mom says made more money than all the other crops they ever raised here. They take them out in the fields in this big wagon, like you'd use for a hayride, and it's supposed to be a big deal that they can eat all they want while they pick. Granddaddy says that nobody can eat enough berries to do you much harm like that.

We help Granddaddy out of the car, and he and I walk over to the tombstones, but Kenny goes right for this big rock sitting like fifty yards off from us that they call the Rock of Ages. Granddaddy says it was the corner of the original McCain land, and that it was mentioned in the first grant one of the Geddies got, back before the American Revolution. He showed me this old piece of paper once, so old that he said when he took it out of his mother's cedar chest after she died that it almost fell apart into nine pieces. Granddaddy had it put back together and laminated, so that you can pick it up and read it without doing any more damage to it. It's as brown as Granddaddy's neck and hands, but you can still read it, and where it says "the old stone corner, next to Locke's Branch," the stone corner is the rock, and Locke's Branch is the ditch.

"It was here when the first white men came here," he tells me, looking toward Kenny and the big rock. "It sure looks like it's going to outlast me."

Granddaddy doesn't know why they call it the Rock of Ages, except that his father called it that and said that had always been its name. The rock is like four feet high, which is maybe three feet eleven inches higher than any of the other rocks I've seen around here. There's nothing but this flat, sandy land anywhere around it, except for the little hill that the cemetery is on. Across the ditch, or branch, or whatever, is the place Granddaddy calls the Blue Sandhills, where the sand is as white as it is at the beach. There's a big lake back there somewhere.

Granddaddy is standing there, resting on his cane, which is sinking into the sand so that he's like leaning to the right. He looks like he's a billion miles away, thinking about something that happened before I was born, I'm sure. It's funny. He can remember stuff from forty years ago, but he can't remember what day it is sometimes.

I go over to where Kenny is. He's picking sandspurs out of his trouser leg, some of those nasty-looking purple ones that'll cure you of wearing shorts down here in about two minutes. He uses the rock to balance with his left hand while he picks them off, one at a time.

"My grandmother used to talk about this rock," he says. "I never saw it till I came up to your granddaddy's one day last year to ask him if I could look around the old place. My great-uncle worked and lived down here until about twenty years ago. Then he went to live with his children until he died."

He rubs the old rock, which is kind of a pinkish-orange color, like it might be magic and he's got three wishes.

"Where do you reckon they got this rock from?" Kenny asks, but it's more like he's really asking himself. "Grand-mother said it was a sacred rock. She said her mother used to find arrowheads and pieces of clay pipes and beads and old-timey Indian stuff buried around it, like people used to worship here a long time ago. Before Jesus saved them from all this," and he gives out a little laugh.

"She said Great-Grandfather took the job sharecropping here because of the rock. Back then, other Indian families would come here to rub it for good luck when they needed some. Didn't work."

He pushes against it, which is about like pushing against a tree. It doesn't begin to budge.

"Some people say it was rolled here from way over in the Piedmont, maybe after our tribe won a battle against another tribe, I don't know. It must've taken a lot of men a long time to roll this thing here. I'd sure love to know why."

It's getting hot as a bitch out in that open field, so we go and get Granddaddy and head back. I ask him later that night if he'd ever heard about the Indians rolling that rock here from somewhere away off. He gets this faraway look in his eyes and gets very quiet.

"Yessir," he says after a while. "I do think Rose told me about that one time. Don't know whether's it's true or not, though."

Rose must be some fifth cousin twice removed I'm supposed to know about.

A week after I get down here, Mom calls. She checked in with the Carlsons, just to make sure the house hadn't burned down, I guess, and they told her about the Great Escape. I don't know if she knows about the shoplifting thing or not, but she knows I flunked English. It's after ten in London, where she says she and Mark the Narc have been pub-hopping. But she seems more concerned than pissed off, wants to know if I'm feeling any better now, how the summer school classes are going, tells me she can't wait to see me in five weeks. She also says that Mark says hi. I guess it was too long a walk around the table to say it himself.

She sent Granddaddy a postcard that got here the day before she called, and she says she'll send lots more now that she knows I'm here, too. Granddaddy gets on for a minute, but he's not much of a talker, especially on the telephone. I'm just getting used to speaking up so he can understand what I'm saying, and the phone lines across the Atlantic aren't exactly like making a call across the street. He hands the phone back to me.

"Justin?" Mom says. "Honey, please look out for your granddaddy, and do what he says. We'll have a long talk when I get back, maybe go away to the beach for the week-end. And don't do anything rash. Things'll get better.''

We hang up, and I'm thinking, Jesus, are things that bad?

School's a snap, and I am having a little bit of fun here, too. We play basketball after classes while I'm waiting for Kenny to get back from his death-defying day with the Future Drivers of America. Winfrey Geddie and his cousin Blue are okay. They call me Cousin Justin, and tell everybody I'm the white sheep of the family. They're both on the Sandy Heath basketball team, and if they don't make it out of summer school, next season is history. They're both about six two already, so the three of us make a mean front line. I only play church league ball back home, but these guys would make anybody look great. They can both dunk, backwards. I can get two inches over the rim, so I could dunk like a marble. There's a three-on-three summer league in Port Campbell, and we're thinking about getting into it.

Mom's always going on about what a waste sports are. She would only let me play soccer when I was little. They have this thing in Montclair called serendipity soccer, which everyone in town calls dip soccer, for good reason. They have leagues for everyone, five to eighty-five, is what they brag about, and the big thing about dip soccer is, like, they don't keep score. Okay, I can see not keeping score in basketball. I mean, after a while, who knows if it's 92–92 or 94–90? But most soccer games I ever played in, the score was either 0–0, 1–0, 1–1 or, if the goalies just didn't show up, maybe 2–1. Now, how the shit are you *not* going to know whether you won or lost when only one goal is scored? Gee, Mom, I don't know who won. We didn't keep score. But we did kick the ball in their goal once, and they didn't kick it in our goal at all. Every five-year-old in Montclair could tell you his team's won-lost record, and I've seen better fights in adult dip soccer games than I've ever seen in football.

In Montclair, only blacks and poor whites play baseball or, God forbid, football. All the university brats, like me, play soccer. If we're like real lucky, our parents let us play basketball between fall and spring soccer. Dad and I would throw the football around when he still lived with us, and the kids in the neighborhood would play tag football in the street. I tell you what: Maybe football's the inhuman, brutal-izing thing Mom says it is, but it's about five times more fun than soccer.

The thing about Winfrey and Blue is, I don't think these guys are ever going to be pestered by the Rhodes scholarship people, even if they never touch a basketball again. And if they can manage to stay in school for the next two years, maybe somebody will give them some kind of college schol-arship to play. Maybe they won't graduate, but they'll be there, anyhow, and maybe something will seep through. I know this much: Winfrey and Blue will be making tires at Kelly-Springfield, or dealing drugs, in less than two years if they don't have basketball. True fact.

I'm their tutor, sort of unofficially. They live over in Old Geddie, which used to be Geddie, according to Granddaddy, but I've never gotten that straight. Anyhow, that's where most of the black people around here live now. Sometimes I go over there, and sometimes they come over here to Granddaddy's and we study on the porch. There aren't many blacks in Montclair. Mom's always telling me how badly they were treated in what she calls "the real South," which she says starts in Richmond, how our own family had had slaves and all, but we've never lived in a neighborhood with even one black family. I guess they just prefer those unpainted little houses over by the railroad tracks. Right.

Winfrey and Blue talk about "axing" questions and wonder if they're ever going to "gradurate," but that isn't exactly the kind of thing you correct in someone else's house, especially since everyone in both their families talks the same way. If everybody in my family said "ax" all the time, that's probably what I'd say, too. It'd be almost disrespectful not to. But I can see where they aren't exactly turning on to the stuff we're reading now. I mean, *Lord Jim*? I can't get into that too much myself. Mom says literature gets better in college, where they let you read things that have been written since the invention of fire. Blue and Winfrey, though, can lay down a line of rap about five minutes long. Too bad they don't give grades on rap. They'd be tutoring me.

Granddaddy gets along with Blue and Winfrey. Blue's father worked at the plywood plant that used to be in Geddie, he said. He refers to them as "colored folks" when they're not around. At least he doesn't call them "niggers" like about everybody else around here seems to. We go to church every Sunday morning, and last week we were out front afterward. That's where people seem to do most of their socializing around here. And I'm standing next to Granddaddy, who's talking with two old guys who are also elders in the church. They're talking about this "nigger" who used to play for North Carolina, and it's "nigger" this and "nigger" that, except that Granddaddy uses "colored" instead. Around here, I guess that makes him a liberal. He doesn't say "colored" in front of Blue and Winfrey, although I guess they're probably used to worse.

CHAPTER SIX

August 8

Not too long ago, Miss Effie Horne come to my house one afternoon. Miss Effie left East Geddie in 1937, when she was about twenty years old. She didn't have much family, and what she had didn't give her much showing. I think she lived with an aunt she didn't get along with. I used to buy her Cokes at the store when she was a young-un, because she seemed so pitiful.

So when she got a chance to go to California to live with some relatives out there, she left and never came back. But here she was, fifty years later, with one of her daughters driving her. Said she'd got the daughter to fly across the country with her, to Raleigh, so they could come down here and see the place where she growed up before she got too old to travel. And I reckon I'm one of the few folks still around that she remembered from back then.

I made them some iced tea and we sat on the back porch under the ceiling fan. Miss Effie and me, we talked about old times, and her daughter would look at her watch every ten minutes or so. I offered to put them up for the night, but the daughter said they already had reservations at the Motel 6 out by the Raleigh-Durham airport.

I never have been much of a talker, and when Miss Effie and her daughter got to arguing about how far it was from where they lived to the Pacific Ocean, I picked up the paper without thinking, pulled out the sports section and turned to page three to see how the Minnesota Twins had done last night. I had read the three or four paragraphs the *Post* saw fit to grace me with when I looked up to see Miss Effie staring at me, and her daughter staring at her.

"Why, Littlejohn McCain," Miss Effie said. "You can read!"

The first thing I remember is Momma's clock. Daddy bought it for her for Christmas in 1897 with the money he made selling a couple of hogs. It sat on the mantelpiece over the fireplace for near-bout sixty years, until Momma died in 1955 and Lex took it down and toted it up to the attic. We just brought it back down again three years ago.

When I wasn't more than four years old, maybe three, I can remember just sitting there on the floor, looking at that big old clock with all the wooden curlicues and that big gold pendulum swinging back and forth, back and forth. Momma used to say that if I was being contrary, all she had to do was put me in front of that old clock, and I'd hush right up. She said sometimes she'd leave me and come back in a hour, and I'd still be perched right there, watching the minute hand catch the hour hand. The funny thing is, after we got it fixed and running and put back on the mantel, behind the oil heater, I'd catch myself doing the same thing. I reckon babies and old folks are all that's allowed to just sit and watch time fly.

Daddy would work all day in the field during good weather. He'd come back in for dinner at noon. Even without a watch, Momma said he never missed by more than five minutes. He'd be hot and tired, and she'd have biscuits and ham and butter beans and rice and gravy. And you had better not of started eating until Daddy got there. When I was four, Lex was fifteen, probably just starting to be a lot of help in the fields. Gruff was twelve and was mainly supposed to fetch water and such. Connie was fifteen, too, of course, and she did as much around the house as Momma did. Century was ten. It was her job to fix the beds and shell peas and beans.

Lafe was seven then. He was already in school, and he would show me the little red reader that the first graders used. They only went to school from late fall until planting time back then, and only Lafe and Century finished all eleven years. I'd look at that reader and see all the letters, and I couldn't wait until somebody showed me the secret that would make all them lines and circles and squirls mean something.

It didn't take but thirty-six more years for that to happen.

Daddy didn't have much time for us until after all the crops was in. He'd lay down for a hour after dinner, then go right back out to the fields again, taking Lex and Gruff with him. He'd be covered from head to foot with old blue overalls and a brown long-sleeved shirt and a straw hat. He had great big hands, the only part of him that the sun got to, and they was covered with freckles and moles and skin cancers that Doc McNeil'd cut off once in a while.

At night after supper, Momma would read to us from the Bible. Sometimes, right after a specially good revival meeting, she'd decided that we ought to be better Christians, and we'd have this big prayer, while we was still at the table. Everybody would have to say something, and it had better of been good, or Momma would make you read the Bible to her for half an hour while she washed dishes. One time she caught me slipping collards back into the bowl during prayer, because I couldn't stomach collards, and she like to of wore me out.

Daddy was old when I was born. I can remember him at seventy-five, still out there plowing, except by that time, Lex and Lafe and me was doing most of it, along with Rennie Lockamy's family that had took over the old cabin where Aunt Mallie and them lived. Rennie's folks claimed to be Lumbee Indians, and we was charitable enough to let them be what they said they was.

Gruff went off to World War I and never really did live here again. He come back long enough to help us paint the whole outside of the house in the summer of, I reckon, 1920, then headed south. He made a good life for him and his family in Atlanta, and he has lots of grandchildren living all around there today. Gruff was one of those folks that seem to be born in the wrong place and has to go out and look for the right one. I reckon he found it.

Daddy would tell us stories about the war, and I've heard Century say many's the time that she wished to goodness she'd wrote down some of that stuff. 'Course, with Daddy, you didn't want to take it as gospel just because he said it. Daddy could stretch things a little. There was no denying, though, that wooden stump from the knee down where he lost his left leg.

He said he was at Gettysburg, but Sara told me years later that if he come home wounded when he was supposed to of, that he must of commuted to Pennsylvania.

Sometimes, it seemed like to me that Daddy wasn't sure himself where he was fighting during the time he was gone. The story he liked to tell the best, though, was about the Geddie boys spittin' in old Sherman's eye. At least, that's the way Daddy saw it. The way he told it, we was always kind of hazy about what happened when the Yankees come to Geddie on their way back north. Sometimes, he'd say him and his daddy and the rest planned a ambush ahead of time. Other times, he'd say he just lifted his gun up and fired it and started all the trouble.

They come right by here on the way to the Blue Sandhills, the Yankees right behind them, and they hid there until the next morning, when they went north to try and ambush them on the Mingo Road, after the Yankees had burnt up everything. But they was too late. Probably just as good, anyways. There wasn't many of them home guard boys left by then, and they was all either too old, too young or too lame. There wasn't much to do but go home and rebuild.

"When we got to Geddie Station," he'd say, talking about what's Geddie itself now, "the smoke was hanging in the air, and we could see that they'd ruint the railroad and burnt down the station. Mr. Gib Carter was standing alongside the road. He was real old, maybe eighty-five. And he was crying, which was peculiar, because Mr. Gib was a tough old bastard, had to be dragged off his horse by his two daughters to keep him from riding with us. And Mr. Gib said, 'Ain't no need to go farther, boys. Geddie's gone.' We could see this real thick smoke rising to the east, and it turned out to be the sawdust pile, which caught fire when they burnt down our sawmill. And there wasn't nothing left here. They even burnt down the washhouse and smokehouse and the two barns. One of them had hitched his horse to the grapevine that Momma planted in 1847 and pulled that down. Pa said he sure was glad she hadn't lived to see that. We had it back up by next summer."

He said it took all the summer just to build a kitchen and big room for everybody to sleep in, and that the house wasn't like it was when I come along for at least six years.

Daddy told that story right many times, and while Century wished she had it all in writing, it didn't bother me. They say that when somebody goes blind, that the other senses all double to make up for it, kind of God's way of making allowances. Well, maybe that's why I can remember things so good.

. . .

In primer and first grade, it hadn't been much of a problem. We would see the letters on the board and recite them all together. Momma seemed concerned that I wasn't picking it up as fast as Lafe and Century did, but she didn't have much time to fret about it.

But then, in the second grade, I got Miss Beulah Bullard. Miss Bullard expected you to be able to read out of the book, and write. It looked simple enough when the other younguns did it, but to me, all them letters might as well of been in Egyptian. I would watch her write letters in chalk up on the board, and then I'd try to do the same thing, but sometimes the "b" would come out "p" or the "m" would be a "w" or worse. Miss Bullard would take my hand in hers and lead my pencil along the right lines, but when she left me to do it myself, it'd get all turned around, and she'd get wrong with me.

It didn't help any that Momma and my first-grade teacher had, between them, made me right-handed, sort of. Ever since I could first throw a rock at a cat, I had been left-handed, something Momma and Daddy hoped I'd grow out of. But when it come time to start school, and I was still using the wrong hand, they couldn't ignore it anymore. Being left-handed, back then, was looked on as something between retarded and sinful. So Momma made me use my right hand at home and Miss Carter, my teacher, made me use it at school. Problem was, I wasn't real good with my right hand. Walking down the swamp road that Daddy and them cut when they started to using the swamp for farmland, headed for the old school on the Ammon Road, I'd throw rocks left-handed at squirrels when we passed the little stand of woods by the Lockamy place, then throw dirt clods into the water at Lock's Branch the same way, then go into the schoolhouse and pick up my pencil from my desk with my left hand and put it in my right. By the second grade, I had got used to it, but my writing was what Momma and Miss Bullard called chicken scratch. Sometimes, when I wasn't sure which way the letters or numbers was supposed to go, I would make it as hard to read as I could, hoping Miss Bullard wouldn't be able to tell if it was right or wrong.

The worst was my name. To me, all the letters looked just alike, and when I would see it wrote out for me, it was like everything was spinning and out of order. One day, I might write LILTTJNOH, and the next it might be LTTIJHN, or LITIEJON. Miss Bullard would make us write our names on the blackboard, just to torment me, I thought. Oh, how I wished I'd of been a Tom or a Ed, although I even spelled Tom "Tow" sometimes. But standing up there at that board, with them other young-uns sniggering behind me and me feeling the heat from Miss Bullard's eyes on me from the side, my brain would just ache trying to see it right in my mind.

"Littlejohn cain't write his own name," I heard my hateful cousin Flossie half whispering behind me more than once.

Miss Bullard sent a note home to Momma and Daddy, and Momma took extra time in the evening, when she might of been praying, to work with me. But Momma couldn't read and write real good either, and when I would keep on getting it wrong, she would get mad at me, and I would cry. Finally, she turned me over to Century and Lafe. The worst, though, was when we'd have prayer together after supper and she would ask Jesus to please forgive me for being so willful and to show me the light so I might follow it and learn.

Understand, East Geddie in 1913 wasn't hardly a hotbed of learning. Most folks, like their mommas and daddies before them, would stick with it long enough to be able to read and write and cipher. Some went through all eleven grades, like Century and Lafe, but it was mostly the girls. The point was to get enough learning so that somebody else wouldn't be able to cheat you.

Century and Lafe would take turns working with me, and they'd get right hot with me, too, when it looked like I wasn't ever going to learn how to do the stuff that come easy to them. I failed the second grade, which wasn't easy to do back then. The only thing I am thankful for, looking back on it, is that there wasn't as much school to go to then as there is now, only about a hundred days a year.

It was Lafe that got me through the second grade second time around, and the third and fourth, for that matter. He'd teach me to memorize things. He might of been the only one in the family that didn't think I wasn't quite right, because he knew I could memorize whole pages of books. Since the same books got used from year to year, I could learn enough from what Lafe read to me to be able to stand up in class and, long as the teacher didn't change anything, pretend to read. It got so, after a while, that I really thought I was reading. I learned the multiplication tables, and teachers got so they knew that something wasn't quite right with me, but that if they asked me, "Littlejohn, what is six times seven?" instead of writing the problem on the board, I could get it.

But the plain, hard truth is that after the fourth grade, and five years of school, I couldn't write my own name. Of course, my spelling was awful, too, and somebody'd have to read the stuff off the blackboard to me, so I would try and sit next to somebody I could trust not to make fun of me or make me feel more stupid than I already felt by telling me the wrong thing. Momma was always on me about the bad grades I got, but, like anything else, if you live with it long enough, it gets to seem normal. I got so I hated books because they made me look so dumb and feel so bad, and whenever there was a chance to help Daddy in the fields instead of going to school, school didn't stand a chance. When I could get Lafe to write me a note, I'd skip altogether, but this was risky business, because half of the teachers went to Geddie Presbyterian like we did, and they was just as like as not to come up to Momma or Daddy on Sunday and ask if Littlejohn was feeling better. Lafe got one of the worst beatings he ever got when my fourth-grade teacher caught him and me forging an excuse note and told Daddy.

But somehow I kept passing. My fifth-grade teacher, Miss Hattie Draughon, fixed that.

Miss Hattie was actually Momma's first cousin, practically family, but she didn't cut nobody no slack. I knew from Century and Lafe that she wasn't going to let me slide, and she lived up to my worst fears on the very first day. We didn't start school till all the tobacco was in, but it was still mighty hot, everybody sweating and ill, just hoping to get our books and get out of there. But Miss Hattie kept us the whole day, longer than the other grades, and about two o'clock, after everybody had ate their lunches outside, the boys sitting together under the big sycamore tree out by the Ammon Road, she told us she wanted us to write two hundred words about what we did over the summer, before we left that day.

Well, one person could of told you what they did that

summer in East Geddie just as good as another'n could of. We worked. We plowed. We suckered tobacco. We cropped tobacco. We barned tobacco. We cured tobacco. We raised and picked cotton. There wasn't anybody in East Geddie going on no European vacations.

Miss Hattie, of course, knew this. She'd lived there already sixty-some years. But she said we'd have to do all two hundred words before we left school.

Some of the girls got through in a half hour. Then the boys started to leave, and by 3:15, there wasn't nobody there but Sammy Tolar and me, and Sammy Tolar was about half retarded. Finally, even Sammy turned in some bunch of nothing, and it was just me and Miss Hattie.

She hadn't expected to be staying much if any past 3:00, and here it was 3:25. She went back to my desk and took the paper I was pretending like I was working on away from me.

"Littlejohn McCain, what in the world is this mess?" she asked. I had never, in five years of school, had to write more than a sentence, and that right off the blackboard.

"This will not do, young man," she went on. "I know your momma and daddy, and they expect better from you than this."

She finally let me go, but she told me I better have that two hundred words done when I got there the next morning. That night, Lafe was in an ill mood, and he wouldn't help me. I sat there until Momma made me go to bed, trying to somehow wish them words on the paper, I reckon.

The next day, first thing, Miss Hattie called me to the front to give her my paper. I took that long walk up to her desk and give her the messiest paper she'd probably ever seen.

She looked at it, turned it sideways, then turned it upside down, while my face was burning up and the children behind me was laughing and giggling like it was Christmas.

"Littlejohn," she said, "I want you to go to that black-board there and show us all how you write your ABCs." And she ripped the paper I'd give her in half.

I started doing what I only hoped was my ABCs, but by the time I got to C, I knew I was in trouble. I kept going, hoping she would stop me and let me go back to my seat, but she kept telling me to keep writing. With the tears welling up, I got as far as N before I just stopped. No matter what she said to me, I wouldn't go no farther.

"Littlejohn, you're going to get a beating," she said, tapping her ruler, and finally she took me out in the hall, this big old board in her hand. She whaled the tar out of me, then made me go back inside and move my desk to the dunce's corner.

"That desk is going to stay there until you learn how to read and write," she said. "I don't have time to teach fifth graders how to read."

Every blessed day she'd send me up to the board, and every day I would mess up the ABCs a different way. She'd have little Alice Fay Cain, who had skipped a grade and weren't hardly nine years old, almost three years younger than me, go to the board to show me how to do it, and that really got everybody to laughing.

Momma and Daddy knew what was going on, because Miss Hattie would give them a report every Sunday at church, and they made Lafe work with me, but Lafe knew what a hopeless case it was, and his heart just wasn't in it.

My last day of school was November 16, 1917. I remember the date because it was the same day Gruff went off to the Army. Miss Hattie brought in these three teachers from Port Campbell that was here for the day just to observe.

"Littlejohn," she called to me from my seat in the corner, "I want you to show these here ladies how you write your ABCs."

After being the class fool for a month, I had got used to the other young-uns laughing, and I could still whip any boy that made fun of me on the playground at recess, so things was tolerable. But here was these women I didn't even know, all dressed up and looking at me like I didn't have no more feelings than a potato bug or something. I was about to "h," although you couldn't tell it from looking at it, I'm sure, when I looked over at Miss Hattie, and she was trying to keep from laughing.

Now, I had endured Miss Hattie's wrath, even a beating now and then, but right then I knew she didn't really care whether I ever learnt to read and write or not, that she was just a mean person that was actually enjoying tormenting me. I didn't throw down the chalk and run out of the schoolhouse crying, like I had done twice before and got took to the woodshed back home for it. I turned around real slow, looked right square at Miss Hattie and said, "I ain't doing this no more, Miss Draughon. I'm fixing to leave now." And I walked out.

It was the first time I had ever sassed a grown person, and I knew it was going to cost me. I got back to the house just before dinner, but of course I couldn't go in, and I'd left my lunch back at the school, so I hid in the near woods until Lafe and the rest come home. He was walking with Annie Williams, who was in the ninth grade, too, and I had to catch him down by Rennie's house to tell him what happened, which of course he had already been told five times by the other young-uns.

He talked me into telling Momma and Daddy before Miss Hattie got to them. She might walk all the way to our house with news this good.

It was a sad time at supper that night, with Gruff gone and all. It was the first time that I could recall that one of our family was gone and not coming back anytime soon. Lex and Connie still lived at home, and folks already was figuring that neither one of them might ever get married. Century worked as a bookkeeper down at the lumber yard, although, unbeknownst to us, Maurice Bunce already had took a shine to her and would marry her within the year. And Lafe had nearbout three years of high school left.

We all prayed for Gruff, and there was a lot more heart in it than in the usual prayers we had to say at supper. Gruff seemed to live up to his name more and more all the time, and him and Momma fought a lot. One time he said ''shit'' and she chased him all the way around the house, twice, with her old sedge broom turned around so that she could conk him on the head with the hard end of it. Everytime she hit him, a little spray of broom straw would come flying up. But Gruff was good-hearted. He'd give us pennies to buy candy at Dawson Autry's store, and nobody loved a good joke any better.

So, with everybody feeling blue about Gruff and all, it wasn't a good time to tell them I wasn't ever going back to school again. But I could just about hear Miss Hattie's footsteps.

I told Momma and Daddy what happened, with everybody

at the table, hoping for a little mercy. Lafe chimed in, telling them how Miss Hattie made fun of me in front of the other children.

Daddy wasn't any too pleased about it, but he might of bought it if Momma hadn't cut such a shine.

"You are going to keep on going to school until you can read and write," she said, her voice rising with every word. "And I am going to beat you good for talking to Hattie like that. Why, she's my first cousin."

And then Momma started in to crying, probably more on account of Gruff being gone than because of Miss Hattie, who she said later she never liked much anyhow. I didn't sass her right there at the table, but I knew I'd run away and live in the hobo jungle we'd see down by the river on the way to Port Campbell before I'd ever set foot in that classroom again.

For six school days in a row, they'd get me up to feed the chickens and milk our old cow, then we'd have breakfast, and then me and Lafe would go back to our room to dress for school. Lafe would come down all cleaned up and carrying his books, and I'd come down with him, dressed just like I was before we ate.

The first day, Momma couldn't believe her eyes. She'd tell people later how I'd always been such a sweet boy, although it's a good thing she didn't know what all went on with us and the Lockamy children. But now, I was just flat refusing to do something. She got her a switch and wore me out, but I just looked at her and said, "I still ain't going to school, Momma." So she screamed and hollered some more, and then Daddy took me with him down to pull the dried peanuts off the hills where we'd stacked them back in early October.

Me and him worked all day, just sitting and talking while we picked peanuts off the dried bushes and put them in burlap sacks. I told him everything about how bad it was at school, and he told me about his younger brother, Jim, that never did learn how to read and write but had a good mind nonetheless. He said he'd try and help me with Momma.

I took my beating for six school days, with another one thrown in for good measure on Sunday when Miss Hattie refreshed Momma's memory. But on the seventh day, Momma rested.

"Littlejohn," she said, "I am tired of beating you ever morning. If you won't learn, you won't learn." I don't think Momma ever did understand what the problem was. Years later, when it was solved, she always seemed to think of it as a miracle. And maybe it was.

I would run into Miss Hattie from time to time over the years, and the older she got, the more she seemed to like to tell that story about me leaving school, and she acted like she thought right much of me. But I didn't go to her funeral.

CHAPTER SEVEN

August 8

It's funny how, looking back at it, there's whole big chunks of my life I don't remember too much about. Just work, eat and sleep. And then there's places where something seemed like it was happening all the time. My fifteenth and sixteenth years was like that. First Babe Ruth, then the catechism and finally, in the fall of 1922, Lafe dying.

. . .

Momma and Daddy should of been tickled that I quit school, because it meant one more full-time hand around the farm during the fall and winter and early spring. With Lafe still in school and Gruff gone to war, there was me and Daddy, plus Amos Lockamy, the tenant farmer, and his two oldest boys. Rennie was my age, and he was still at Indian school. It tore Momma up that a Indian boy was going to learn more from books than I did.

Rennie and me, we was close when we was little. Rennie'd meet me down in the near woods between our house and his, and we'd play hide-and-go-seek or throw rocks at squirrels or play in the crop ditch, where Daddy and Rennie's daddy was trying to bring some of the water from the swamp to the near fields for irrigation. But when I was seven, Momma told me I wasn't to play with Indian children no more. I hadn't even thought of Rennie as being any different until then. It would of been hard for our parents to keep us from getting together, but Rennie's folks told him the same thing, probably after Daddy talked to his daddy, and we just kind of drifted apart, so that by the time we was eleven, we'd work together in the summer, drink from the same pail, share the same watermelon and then turn and go our separate ways at quitting time without ever thinking about it. When Rennie died, near-bout ten years ago, I did go to his funeral, but we wasn't close.

Anyhow, while the other children was at school, we'd be working around the farm, which was fine with me. Anybody around here'll tell you I ain't ever been afraid of work. Working hard made me feel important, like I was worth something, which was not a feeling I ever got at school.

In October, before the first frost, we'd dig Irish potatoes

and saw and chop wood to build up a supply for the winter. Then we'd pick the last corn, take it to the barn and shuck it. Some of it would be took to the mill to be ground into grits and cornmeal, some was fed to the hogs and chickens and some was fed to the mules, whole. Then we'd cut the stalks for fodder.

Before Thanksgiving, we'd do hog killing, which took up the better part of a week. We'd get old Babe McNeill, a colored man that lived down in Old Geddie, to come over and take charge. Babe knew how to kill hogs, how to dress them to get the most meat out of them. The smell of a hog killing is like nothing I ever smelt at that time. But there was some good eating between Thanksgiving and Christmas, with all the fresh sausage and ham and liver puddin' and scrapple and chitlins. There'd be enough to last just about the whole year, but by October, we'd be starting to run low, so hog killing was something of a celebration, after you got over the smell of it.

We'd try to get all the repairs to the house and barn done in November, too. One of the barns was built right after Sherman burnt all Captain McCain's old barns to the ground. It seemed like it was old in 1917, but now it looks like it's going to outlive me. There was always boards to be replaced and fence to be fixed around the chicken yard and hog pen.

The hatefullest job, though, to me, was cutting ditch bank. We'd have to go along Locke's Branch, the whole length of the farm, half a mile, cutting all the reeds out, using a bush ax. It was always cold when we done it, and we'd always get wet. We'd spend the whole day out there and maybe go two hundred yards with four of us at it. Then when we got done with the branch, we'd have to do the crop ditch, all the way over to the near fields. All summer I'd see them reeds building up around the branch and know what was waiting in November.

In November, December and January, we'd hunt some, me with the Iver-Johnson single-shot 12-gauge that Daddy bought me, the one I give away in 1922. We wouldn't usually have time to take the whole day and go into the Blue Sandhills hunting deer until after Christmas, except for Saturdays. I think that from the time I was eleven until I stopped hunting, we shot two deer. But there was lots of squirrels and rabbits then.

By February, it was time to plant the tobacco beds and start the whole thing over. We'd break up the land in early March and plant Irish and sweet potatoes not long after. Daddy always said, plant stuff that grows underground in the dark of the moon, stuff that grows above ground in full moon. That might sound like a lot of bull to some, but it seemed like it worked.

Lex would work down at the lumber yard in the winter, helping run things. We was out of the sawmill business by then, never really did much with it since I was born, but the Godwins had started their big operation down by the mill-pond, had already run their tram tracks from the pond up to the Campbell and Cool Spring line at McNeil. Soon as they built the tram, it was the favorite place to hunt deer, because there was about a fifty-foot gap cut in the thicket. The tram had this one little engine and about six flat cars where they'd stack the pines and ship them to McNeil, where the main office of Godwin's was, and there they'd cut them up and ship them out on the train.

Back then, there was bobcats down there, and every once

in a while, somebody would shoot a bear. Daddy said that before I was born, a bear chased one of Aunt Mallie's nephews all the way up to their house. They claim there ain't any alligators north of South Carolina anymore, but I saw this:

There was a Hittite named Jake Formy-Duval that worked in the logging camp at the millpond. He had one of the little cabins that was there for single men. He had come from deeper in the sandhills, a place called Kinlaw's Hell, where all the Hittites come from, and he would trap for beaver when he wasn't logging. One day, he come back with a alligator. This gator was maybe five feet long, and Jake Formy-Duval had somehow managed to chain it to a tree not too far from the camp. Nobody knew where he got it, but he'd feed that gator, which would eat just about anything, on whatever he shot or trapped. I was about six when Daddy took me and Lafe down there to see it. There was a dozen or so men standing in a little pine clearing near the water, in a circle. We got closer, and there was this gray scaly log with eyes that didn't pay us no attention a-tall. We got as close as we dared to, moving ahead about a inch at a time, when this squinty-eyed, black-haired fella with bad teeth grabbed me from behind.

"Time to feed the gator," he yelled as he picked me up. He held me in the air over the gator for a few seconds before Daddy made him put me down and threatened to cut him. The gator didn't last but about a month before some drunks turned him loose and they had to shoot him. Daddy said a man who was supposed to know how to count alligator years said that one was more than a hundred years old.

The years after I quit school until 1922 wasn't bad years, not looking back on them now, at least. I worked alongside

Daddy and the other men until he fell and broke his hip after
Lafe died. After that, he mostly did what he could around the
house and barns. But we'd work hard all day and play hard
on Saturday afternoons and in the pink of the evening.

Baseball had just come to be a big thing around Geddie.
In March of 1921, Daddy let us off from plowing so me and
Lafe could ride in the wagon with some of the other young
folks to Port Campbell to see Babe Ruth. He had hit fifty-
some home runs the year before for the Yankees, and they
was heading north to start the season. They was supposed to
play a game against the semipro team in town. Babe Ruth
might of been the only name most of us knew in baseball,
that and Shoeless Joe Jackson.

There was a ball park then on a piece of bottom land right
by the Campbell River, next to the bridge. The game was at
two o'clock, but by noon they said all the stands around
home plate was filled up, and men and boys was standing four
deep along the foul lines, all the way to the six-foot board
fence. The river bank was right behind the fence; the flood
washed it away the next year.

We had got a late start because the McNeils, who we was
riding with, never could be anywhere on time. When we got
there, about one o'clock, you couldn't get nowhere near the
field. The Port Campbell Grays looked like bugs from the
river bridge, and the Yankees were this little-bitty patch of
lint over by the bench area on the first-base side.

"Come on," Lafe said when we'd crossed. "I got a idea."

Me and him and the McNeils' two boys went around the
field. We had to circle almost back to Water Street to get
around the crowd. We come up the first-base side, on past
the seats. About twenty feet back of the folks that was

standing was this big sycamore tree with long white branches like ghost arms going out every which way. One branch, which caught Lafe's eye from all the way up at the bridge, went level with the ground and about ten feet high, until it near-bout reached the field itself.

"That's where we'll be sitting," Lafe said, pointing up there.

Jack McNeil was afraid to climb up and went to try and worm his way through the crowd. Me and Lafe and Jack's brother Leonidas went to the trunk and started to climbing. Lafe gave us both a leg up, him being the oldest, and then he climbed up to the branch on his own. We crawled way out to about five feet from the edge and perched there on our limb like three crows on a clothesline. We wasn't but about twenty-five feet from the Yankees' bench. I can remember feeling like Zacchaeus in the Sunday School song, where he can't see, so he climbs up in the sycamore tree, and Jesus sees him up there and invites himself to Zacchaeus' house.

Well, Babe Ruth didn't exactly come home with us for dinner. We was all three yelling and hollering his name, and because the noise was coming from a direction he hadn't expected, I reckon, we got his attention.

He looked up and gaped at us yelling and screaming. It was just before the game, and the Yankees had been taking batting practice, knocking clean white baseballs we'd of killed for over the fence and into the river. People was out there in rowboats. A man drowned that day when he fell out of his boat trying to catch a ball before it hit the water.

Babe Ruth walked over to the branch where we was sitting and looked up at us. He wasn't a fat man a-tall, not then anyway, but he had this round face that made him look that way, and he had this funny little walk, with his toes turned in. Lafe noticed next spring that every player on the Grays had suddenly turned pigeon-toed.

Babe Ruth looked up, right at us, his eyes all streaked with red veins.

"Kid," he said, looking right at me, because I was the farthest out on the branch, "if you don't shut the fuck up, I'm gonna take this bat and knock you over the fuckin' fence." Everybody got real quiet around us, not out of respect or fear, 'cause Babe Ruth wasn't nothing but a ballplayer, but out of shock. Folks around here would give their young-uns a switching in a heartbeat, and men might let a "hell" or "damn" slip now and then, but to use that word to boys, with even a few ladies present, didn't set too well.

"Don't you worry, boys," come this voice from the crowd after what seemed like five minutes but was probably more like thirty seconds. "Ain't no Yankees going to mess with you."

It turned the crowd against the Yankees, who was hardly a favorite to begin with in a town that still had living Civil War veterans. They beat the Grays 21-2, and Babe Ruth hit a home run to right field that landed close enough to the other side of the river that a fella was able to find it in the shallows. They said it went near-bout seven hundred feet, but they might of exaggerated a little bit. That ball's in the Scots County Museum now.

They booed the Yankees when they left, although some folks did try and get autographs. It was the last time they stopped over in Port Campbell. We never told Momma and Daddy, partly because we was afraid they'd never let us go watch a baseball game again, and partly because they'd want to know what the word was that Babe Ruth said. We made the McNeil boys promise not to tell, too, and Momma never did hear the whole story until after Daddy died.

I never did have no use for Babe Ruth after that.

I wasn't what you would call real religious, but it made Momma happy to see me at least go to church, since school was over. By the time I was fifteen, I had a bass voice that would get deeper for a couple more years and cause me to be in the church choir, where I still sit on occasion, although my voice is about gone like the rest of me. Momma used to say she got goose bumps hearing me come in on "up from the grave he arose" when we'd sing "He Arose" at Easter sunrise service.

It was the catechism that convinced me that I wasn't retarded. Momma had tried near-bout forever to get first Century and then Lafe to learn the child's catechism at church. They'd start in on it for a while, then quit, then start again. Now, they were way too old for it, and I was fifteen, almost too old. But over the years, I had picked up about half of it just listening to Lafe and Century. So all that spring, I would get Lafe to read the question, and then the answer, and I would memorize the answer. There was about 170 questions, as I recall, and by May I had every one of them down pat. We hadn't told Momma, because we didn't want to disappoint her again. Nobody from our church had memorized the child's catechism in ten years, and it would mean a lot to her if one of her young-uns did it.

So, I went over to McNeil one Saturday afternoon. I interrupted Reverend Winstead, that served our church and two more, while he was preparing his sermon, but when he found out what I was there for, he took me into his little study. It smelt like pipe tobacco, books all over everywhere.

"I thought you couldn't read, Littlejohn," he said. "How did you learn the catechism?"

I told him I memorized it, just like I did all them hymns we sung. He shrugged his shoulders to let me know he didn't expect much. Then he said a prayer, and then he started asking the questions. I near-bout slipped up on "What is sin?" which is a long answer that I couldn't tell you now to save me. But when it was over, he had to agree that I'd done it.

They made the announcement on Mother's Day, had me come down out of the choir and get the Bible with my name on it in gold. I still got it. Momma didn't know a thing about any of it until the preacher called me forth to the pulpit, because I had asked him not to tell anybody. It made me as proud as anything that had happened to me in my life.

After church, everybody come up to congratulate me and look at the new Bible. Finally, I got to Momma. She was crying a little.

"Son," she said, "Jesus must have a plan for you, or He wouldn't of give you the power to learn all that."

Now, what I wanted to ask her, when I thought of it, was this: If Jesus got all the credit for me learning the catechism, how come I got all the blame for doing so bad in school? But at least Momma was treating me a little less like something that wasn't quite good enough, whether she give the credit to me or Jesus.

Lafe's dying was something I shut out for a long time after. Hunting accidents happened all the time around here, but to shoot and kill your own brother, and best friend, is something I am not sure I ever have quite got over. The times I prayed to the Lord to make it all a dream, let me wake up and find Lafe laying in the next bed, or to just put me back there, the split second before I pulled the trigger. But it never done any good.

Georgia used to tease me all the time about saying "Be careful" every time she did anything, said it ought to be our family motto. But she didn't know, maybe still don't, the evil that comes from just being careless.

CHAPTER EIGHT

August 8

The day after Lafe's funeral, we went back to cutting ditch bank.

It was a Tuesday, so we was already behind because of the burial, and Daddy said there wasn't any sense in wasting good weather. It was still warm enough to be enjoyed by them that could, not yet hog-killing time by any means, even though Thanksgiving was near-bout on us.

Lex was working in the lumber yard, so it was me and Daddy and the Lockamys, five of us out there. We had cleared past their house and was headed for the corner, down where we put in the strawberry patches in 1956. Nobody give much thought to the cemetery, maybe because we had come to it the day before from the Ammon Road, going through East Geddie from the church. But when we walked along the branch, headed north to the spot where we had quit working on Friday, we could see the colors up on the little ridge. Everything else in the country is just shades of brown and gray in November, so the flowers by the new-dug grave—the tombstone wouldn't be there for a week or so—caught your eye right off. We all knew, without anybody saying anything, that we'd be working right by it all day, headed up to the Rock of Ages. If we cut two hundred yards, we'd be there, working right by the cemetery on the little rising looking out over the Blue Sandhills, by dark.

Daddy was old by then. He'd passed seventy-eight in April and wouldn't plow another row after he fell working on the roof Momma told him to let somebody else do, the week before Christmas. He looked at the graveyard and said, without looking at anybody—surely not at me—"I reckon we'd be better off cutting the crop ditch today."

So we went back in the other direction and spent the next five days bush-axing the crop ditch through to the near fields. By the time we was ready to pick back up on Lock's Branch toward the graveyard, Daddy told me at breakfast to just go on without him.

He never talked to me about it, and I never talked to him, after I had told him how sorry I was, how I wished it was me instead, the day it happened. Maybe he didn't blame me, but he sure didn't forgive me, either. We just didn't look at each other much anymore, and we tried not to be alone with each other. Lafe looked just like him, and even though Lex was the oldest and Gruff was going to be the richest, I always thought, even before, that Daddy felt like Lafe would be the one to make him proud.

Lafe was bright as a dollar, and smart. Around here, you might ought to know, smart don't mean you're a genius; it means you work like a mule, even without nobody telling you to. It comes in right handy on a farm. I was smart, but nobody much back then ever accused me of being extra bright. Lafe was both. Things was booming after the war, and Daddy was hoping to be able to send him to the Presbyterian Academy over in Pineland, on the other side of Cool Spring, in another year, maybe even see a lawyer in the family before he died.

In May of 1927, when Daddy was going fast after he had his big stroke, I'd sit by the bed holding his hand when Momma needed a rest, and sometimes he'd try to talk. He pretty much still had his right mind, but the stroke had messed him up so he couldn't make himself understood, and that would aggravate him so bad he'd cry sometimes

One morning, about ten o'clock, I was holding his hand and he seemed like he was sleeping, when all of a sudden, he opened his eyes wide and looked right at me, and it seemed like he hadn't looked at me in years. I was struck by how much his bright blue eyes had faded, to where they didn't hardly have any more color in them than the veins in his hands.

"Afe?" he croaked out.

"No, Daddy," I told him. "It's me, Littlejohn."

"Ere Afe?"

I reckon I could of lied and told him that Lafe would be back directly, just to go on back to sleep, but his mind seemed so good up to that point that I felt like he must of just woke up from a dream and was confused.

"Daddy," I told him, "Lafe ain't here. Lafe died five years ago. In the hunting accident."

Daddy got this look on his face like he was just learning about it for the first time, and I could see his eyes tearing up.

"I'm sorry, Daddy," I told him. "I couldn't help it. I'm sorry."

He closed his eyes, and pretty soon he was sleeping again, or seemed like he was. He was dead six days later, and he never said anything to me again, one way or the other. We put him on the hill next to Lafe and the rest.

The days after Lafe died seemed about a year long each, with the whole thing coming back to me about every five minutes. But somehow, the days became weeks, the weeks months, the months years. I have heard of folks grieving theirselves to death, but I reckon you have to be old to do that. Young folks got too much working against death.

I would go out every morning, Monday through Saturday, to work. I found enough barn work and house repairs to get me through until it was time to plant the tobacco beds, and then farming took over until the next harvest.

Instead of coming back to the house for dinner at noon, I would take some sausage and biscuits or a piece of cheese or a sweet potato and some corn bread out with me and just eat in the field, under the big old oak by the property line if I was working in the near fields, under the sycamores and sweet gums if I was down in the swamp. I'd pump a jug full of water from our pump or the Lockamys' and leave it in the shade. I'd tell Momma not to wait supper for me, and most days I'd manage to get there later and eat by myself, out on the porch in the summertime after everybody else had finished, in the dining room after the rest was through in the winter. It wasn't a good time for talking to people, and we all just kind of kept our distance. Momma never come out there when I was eating by myself in the near fields, where she could see me from the back porch, and asked me to come up and eat with the rest of them, although Lex, bless his heart, did try and get me to from time to time.

What was I thinking about all that time? I could not exactly tell you. Sometimes, I felt like I was talking to Lafe. I know that Rennie would kid me about talking to myself, but it was just that Lafe seemed like he was closer out there in the fields, and sometimes he seemed near-bout alive. In the August heat, I've seen him standing in the shade over by the pin oaks at the edge of the woods, I'll tell you that. I sure didn't tell anybody about it back then, though. I didn't hate myself quite enough to want a one-way ticket to the crazy house at Dix Hill.

The main thing, though, was that, by working hard, I could feel like I was worth something. That always had been my way. Back when most folks thought I was retarded and never would be good for anything, I'd try to make up for not being able to read by outworking everybody on the farm. If I kept at it, kept that ditch bank so clean you could eat out of it, kept the weeds out of the tobacco and corn, got the whole place looking better than it ever had, maybe everybody would forget someday that I'd killed my own brother. Maybe I'd forget, too.

Church was the hardest part. It was the only place where I had to be around a whole bunch of people that knew what I had done, or what they thought I had done, and wasn't family. But not going to church would of made things even worse than they was. So, every blessed Sunday, I would go sing in the choir, then walk back home instead of waiting for the buggy, because Momma and Daddy would want to gab for a while after the sermon, and I didn't have nothing to say to nobody.

I thought about running away but I just couldn't make myself do it. In spite of Lafe, in spite of the silences and the cemetery and everything, this was the only home I had, and I couldn't bear to leave it. It wasn't just Momma and Daddy and them. It was the place itself. I would of been plumb happy never to leave the farm. Don't feel much different now. It always amazes me that Georgia could just pick up and move somewhere different every two or three years after college, how she never seems to care if she ever sees this place again. It never was like that with me.

One time, about 1925, Gruff tried to get me to come down to Atlanta with him. He was already managing a store down there and said it might be good for me to get away from home. I'm sure nobody would of cared all that much, but this is the only place I ever felt comfortable. Maybe if I had been able to read and write, it would of felt different, but I don't think so.

There was days, back then, when I wouldn't say a word to a living soul. I could get up at 5:30, before Momma, cook my own fatback and eggs and biscuits, make a couple of extra biscuits and add some sausage or a sweet potato for dinner, fill up the jug with water, go hitch up old Susie and be in the fields by 6:30. Lex would come out a little bit later with the other mule, Moses, and we'd work all day, Lex going back to the house for dinner and me eating under the shade.

I don't mean to make out like the years from 1922 until 1942 was one long row I plowed. There was times when we'd all get together and talk and laugh some, like before. There was days when it would rain, or days in the winter when not one thing needed doing. It's just that, after a while, there wasn't much need on my part for company. I talked to Lafe's ghost or whatever you want to call it a lot more than I talked to the living.

Neither Lex nor Connie ever did marry. It wasn't all that peculiar a thing back then, not marrying. Miss Hattie Draughon and her two sisters, Miss Corrinne and Miss Jessie, didn't any of them marry, just stayed at their daddy's big house, after their momma died, taking care of each other until none of them could get about and they all had to be sent to the nursing home up on the Mingo Road.

I think it was harder, back then, on the older ones than the younger ones. Lex knew pretty much that he would be taking over the farm some day, so he always was expected to pay more attention to it than Gruff or Lafe when they were boys. He wasn't a bad-looking man when he was young, although he was more bashful than us younger ones, and I reckon we used to tease him a lot. It's funny, but I don't think Lex had a date until he was way past grown, and even then, he would keep it to himself. He'd just go off at night, after we got the car in 1928. Later, when we had to put the car up on blocks because we couldn't afford to run it, he'd walk somewhere or other at night. Nobody would of thought of locking their doors back then, and nobody really knew when Lex come back, but he did wake me up coming in as late as three A.M. some nights.

Connie wasn't as pretty as Century, who had Momma's yellow hair and soft, pretty face. Momma looked like a angel when she was young. I can see that now looking at her pictures. Makes me wonder what she saw in a old, one-legged Civil War veteran like Daddy.

Connie had sharper features, like Lex, a nose like a hawk's, and she was too skinny. I see girls now trying to get as thin as they can, and I remember how, when we was young, a man wanted a wife with some meat on her bones. If you got too skinny back then, they'd ship you off to the TB sanatorium.

There was a fella come to work in Geddie about the time Daddy died, and he started coming around, like a stray dog. His name was Homer Guinn, and he was one of the sons of this trashy Guinn woman that lived down south of here on the Ammon Road. Nobody knew who half of her young-uns' daddies was, and no two of them seemed to have had the same one. But this one, Homer, a boy with slick black hair and a complexion dark enough to suggest the worst, seemed to take a liking to Connie, who already was past being give up for an old maid. And the funny thing was, even though Connie always seemed like she was content to cook and keep house right where she was born, she took a shine to Homer. He started going to the Geddie Presbyterian Church and sitting with her, and they'd spend evenings on the old glider we used to have on the front porch, just talking away. He'd leave about 9:30 and walk back to his momma's.

It all come to an end one day that June. I had walked in from the swamp and unhitched Susie, and I was coming up from the barn. It was near-bout dark, but there was enough light left to see two people standing out by the carhouse we'd built for the Ford. As I got closer, I could see it was Lex and Connie. Lex had a tobacco stick in his hand that he'd picked up off the ground. Connie had the butcher knife.

"I am going to cut you up like a hog!" she screamed at him. She was as mad as a wet settin' hen.

"No, you ain't, Connie," Lex said, and I could tell he was a little nervous. I was about fifty feet away, and she probably knew I was there, but she was just wild. I hadn't seen her lose her temper since she got grown.

"I did it for you, honey," he said as he backed up into the bean rows, being real careful not to trip. "He wasn't no good. I marked them chickens because they been disappearing for weeks. I never said nothing about it because I knew you wouldn't believe me, so I had to get proof."

"You just want me to stay here all my sorry life and cook and wait on you all. And I won't do it. I won't do it! I'd rather cut you up and go to jail with him."

What had happened was that Homer Guinn had been slipping by the chicken coop on the way home and walking off with Momma's white leg'orns, one at a time. Finally, Lex had put little bands on their legs, not like the usual ones, but smaller, hard to see. When he had counted the night before and come up one short, he sent the sheriff over to Miss Guinn's, where they found the chicken amongst hers out in the yard. They didn't keep Homer in jail for long, but Lex let him know he'd be shot if he come sniffing around here again.

Connie cut a shine about it, told Lex she'd wait and catch him when he was sleeping and kill him then, and she didn't go to church for a good six months afterward. Sometimes, Lex looked more tired than usual out in the fields, like maybe he wasn't sleeping good. Connie got over it, though, and she stayed right here for her whole life, waiting on me and Lex and Momma until I got married and moved out, and then Momma died. Then it was just her and Lex. She died in 1968, when she was near-bout seventy-three years old, six days after Lex passed away. It was the only six days of her adult life, I reckon, that she didn't have nobody to wait on. That's probably what killed her.

After Daddy died, I felt more responsible than before toward my family. Other than working, I'd go to church on Sunday and Wednesday night and maybe go down to the store in East Geddie on Saturday afternoon as it got a little easier to be with people. About the only gambling I ever did was over Coca-Colas. I love Coca-Cola; Momma said it was my one vice. But I had this special trick, where I could take one of them seven-ounce bottles like they used to have, that really had some kick to them, and drain one in a single swallow. If they could get anybody that didn't come around the store that much, or somebody that was new in town, they'd get me to bet him I could drink the Coke in one gulp. I remember one time Jack Tatum, who was a farmer just down the road from here, said, "Littlejohn, it's a good thing you don't drink liquor. You'd be a drunk."

And then, of course, there was Rose.

Rennie's momma had her last baby when I was eleven, in 1917. She was this little Indian girl that used to bring us water when we was all working down in the swamp. She wasn't as dark as her brothers and older sister, had kind of a orangish color to her, skin that stayed right tan in the dead of winter and hair that was reddish-blond and curly, but not kinky. She took after the rest of her family so little that lots of people figured she must not of been Amos's, but if he ever thought so, he didn't let on, and he seemed like he was crazier about Rose than any of the rest.

Up past the Rock of Ages another hundred yards or so, into McDaniel property, there used to be a pond, not more than thirty feet across, where us boys would run for a quick swim at dinnertime in the summer. I wouldn't no more do something like that now than I would walk into a fire, with all the cottonmouths and pilot snakes around here, but back in them days, we'd take all our clothes off and jump right in. Some of us, me included, never even learned how to swim, but the pond, it was just a low place where Lock's Branch run out, and it wasn't no more than five feet deep in the middle. Just deep enough to cool off in. They filled it in more than twenty years ago when they cut down all the trees there and started to planting soybeans.

I bet I hadn't been down there in five years or more when, one day in the summer of 1933 when it must of been 100 degrees out and we was working in the swamp, I got this craving to go down there and get wet all over. Rennie and his brothers had gone to the house for dinner, and I was sitting by the sweet gum at the edge of the branch, not a breath of air. You could smell the crops burning.

I followed the branch past the graveyard and on into the thicket where the pond was. I took off my overalls and brogans, my socks and brown work shirt and underwear and jumped right in. I was twenty-seven then, and had thought myself a man for some time, but that water felt so good that I was splashing around like a young-un at the beach.

I never saw Rose until she jumped in right behind me. Scared me to death. I didn't know whether it was a bear or a dog or maybe a gator. I jumped and turned around, ready to fight for my life, and here was this Indian girl, who was practically a baby last time I took notice of her, buck naked and all filled out, right in front of me.

She reached down between my legs, where no woman had reached before.

"If you want me," she said, "you can have me." Plain as that.

And so I did have her, right there in the sand and swamp grass along the edge of our own private play pool. Because Rose didn't have no brothers or sisters anywhere near her age or any friends within a mile, she had pretty much had the pond to herself for the last few years, after the rest of us thought we was too old for such foolishness. She said later that she had never seen another soul there until she followed me down that July day in 1933.

Maybe it's like this with all men. I don't know, because I come from a generation where you won't supposed to kiss and tell. But every woman I have ever been with has known more than me, has led me down that path, starting with sweet Rose. If you had looked at it from outside, not knowing everything, you'd of said, here's this cradle robber taking advantage of this poor little sixteen-year-old Indian girl. He ought to be horsewhipped.

But Rose taught me everything. I was her plaything, not the other way around. I don't know where a girl that age learned such things, but after I got over the shock of sharing myself with another human being after being locked up inside myself for years and years, I was just glad that she had.

Nobody ever talked about anybody being a virgin back then. Everybody just took it for granted that you was, especially if you was a woman but probably if you was a man, too, and there wasn't all this stuff like them *Playboy* and *Penthouse* magazines and X-rated movies to keep people's minds on sex all the time like there is now. People didn't seem to think about it that much, and it probably wasn't all that strange for a old bachelor of twenty-seven like me never to have done it. At least, that's the way it seems to me, looking back.

The hardest thing to do was to keep it quiet. I would go all the way to Lennon's Drug Store in Port Campbell, where I didn't know anybody, to buy rubbers, and then I'd hide them behind a timber in the back of the little workshop me and Lex built behind the carhouse, stopping by to pick up one every time I planned to meet Rose down at the pond.

In warm weather, we'd get together whenever we could. We had this message system. If I was working by myself in the swamp or knew Rennie and his brothers was going to be way off at the other end of the farm where we wouldn't be together at dinner, I'd put this red bandanna around my neck that Rose could see all the way up to her folks' yard. Then, if she could get away, between housework and fixing dinner for the men, she'd tell her momma she was going for a walk. When she got a ways from the house, headed for the pond, she would do the only thing that ever made me remember that she was a Indian. She'd give a mourning-dove call. That was my signal. When I heard the mourning dove, I knew it was time to tie up the mule and head for Rose's pond.

In cold weather, we had another plan. There was a old slave cabin, now long since tore down, back farther in the McDaniel woods, where we could be alone and warm. Sometimes we'd both slip out at night, with her giving a owl hoot as the okay signal, and go do it in the tobacco barn farthest from the house.

We went on like this for five years, and, to my knowledge, didn't nobody ever find out. Lex might of been puzzled that I'd volunteer to work in the swamp, where the air was so heavy and still, so far away from the house, but he was glad for me to do it. And Rose had got so wild and independent as she growed older that her folks, who was getting on in years, just about give up and let her go where she pleased, no questions asked.

It all ended in 1938, one bright blue October morning at the slave cabin. The first frost was barely off the ground. I was supposed to be clearing some of the thorns out of the graveyard and took a chance that nobody would notice that I'd gone into McDaniel's woods. Rose was waiting for me, and she didn't beat around the bush.

"Johnny," she said—that was what she always called me—"I'm going to have a baby."

I started to declare that I'd been careful, when she stopped me.

"Don't worry," she said, "it ain't yours."

I knew that Rose would leave from home sometimes for a week or more, and I didn't fool myself that I was her only lover. But it was a shock to hear that she was carrying another man's child. She said she was two months gone, that her momma and daddy didn't know nothing about it yet. She said she was aiming to marry Gentry Locklear, who she saw now and then, and move in with his people. She didn't love Gentry near as much as she did me, she said.

I could of married her. I know she'd of gone along with it. I could say it might of killed Momma and them, but looking back now, it was pure lack of guts that kept me from marrying that wild, beautiful girl. If it'd been my baby, then I might of said to hell with what people say and married her anyhow. We could of had a pretty good life together, I think. But I was right sure that baby wasn't mine, since we'd been real careful, and I couldn't stand the snickers, didn't think I ever could go back to Dawson Autry's store again on a Saturday afternoon. I was a coward.

Rose and Gentry, who was about Rose's age and a Lumbee like her, did get married, and seven months later, she give birth to this little baby that was lighter-skinned than her even. And you know what she named him? Johnny. Not John. Johnny Little Locklear. I saw her one time when the baby was little, walking down High Street in Port Campbell with her husband by her side. She didn't speak, just looked down at the baby as we passed on the street, looked up at me and winked. Rose never come home much after she got married, and her momma and daddy didn't live much longer. Johnny lived around Port Campbell until he joined the Army. He got killed in Vietnam, left a wife and three young-uns at home.

If I ever had a son, his name was Johnny Little Locklear.

When the Japs bombed Pearl Harbor, I was thirty-five years old, a bachelor that worked hard six days a week, sang bass in the choir on Sunday and saw Belva Culbreth on Sunday nights. Belva was a widow who went to Geddie

Presbyterian, too. After Rose, she was a cold bucket of water, but it looked like everybody expected us to get married, an idea I found no pleasure in.

Lex was the eldest son, and forty-six years old to boot. No way he was going into the Army. I probably could of missed World War II myself, but I didn't want to. If me and Belva had got married, it might of carried some weight, and if they'd come to understand that I couldn't read and couldn't even write my own name real well, that would of done it. But that's not the way it happened.

It would be unfair to Belva to say that I preferred Hitler to her, the way some hateful, spiteful people in our church said I did. What it come down to was duty. Granddaddy had lost his money and Daddy his leg in the Civil War, and Gruff had went overseas in the First World War. I felt like I ought to go. There wasn't any feeling of volunteering for certain death. It was more a feeling of excitement. The only thing I would miss, I knew, was this old farm.

When I went before the selective board in Port Campbell, I already had got some coaching from a couple of boys that hung around the store and couldn't read much better than I could but still managed to get in the Army. I knew what to expect. The biggest problem was my name. For years, I had just signed it L. J. McCain, making such a mess of my last name that folks couldn't tell if I'd spelt it wrong or not. I was still a heavy favorite to get Littlejohn wrong.

So when they asked me my name, I told them L. J. McCain, which was what I had put on the census last time.

They wanted to know what L.J. stood for. I told them it didn't stand for nothing, just L.J. Period. It wasn't totally unheard of. There was people back then that didn't have a name except initials. And the only place my whole name was registered the way it was supposed to be spelt was in the family Bible at Momma's. So, they bought it. They must of known I couldn't read, the mess I made of stuff, but I was a big, healthy farmer, and the U.S. Army wasn't being too picky in early 1942, I don't reckon.

I left in April for basic training, where they give me dogtags reading "L (only) J (only) McCain." For four years, I was either "McCain" or "Eljay."

Why they sent me to cook school, I don't know. I reckon they figured that at my age I'd be a better cook than a fighter, although it seemed to me like I was in better shape than them twenty-year-old city boys that was always complaining about the food.

For me and a lot of other farm boys just out of the Depression, we never ate so good. No more poke salad, no more pork three times a day if you were lucky.

I spent the rest of 1942 and 1943 and part of 1944 in parts of the United States that might as well of been a foreign country to me. We guarded Italian and German prisoners in Texas, helped civilian workers process sugar at a factory in Cairo, Illinois, did desert training in Arizona. It seemed like we never was going to see any fighting. Finally, though, we got our turn. I can remember walking down streets in Brooklyn, New York, waiting to ship out, and the houses would have signs out front: NO DOGS OR SERVICEMEN. There wasn't a day I didn't feel a little homesick. I could always get away back into some dark corner of myself and get by wherever I was, though. I would carry on conversations in my mind with Lafe, and that helped a lot.

We sailed for Marseilles, France, which everybody on the

ship pronounced "Marcells." France was a filthy place. Women going to the bathroom right alongside the road, everything dirty and nasty. Georgia tells me it's a beautiful country now, that she'd live there if she could figure a way to make a living. I must of just caught it at a bad time.

It was the only chance I'd ever had to meet people from all over. My best friend was a crazy Polack from Toledo, Ohio, named Lewandowski. Edward Joseph Lewandowski. Me and him was together from basic on, and old Lewandowski saved me more than once. I wasn't a bad cook, considering what we had to work with, but I couldn't read much better than when I walked out on Miss Hattie's class in 1917. So Ski would read the ingredients to me. He usually didn't have to do it but once, and because I tended to go more on taste than measurements, him and me was able to improve on a lot of the stuff. He helped me through cook school, and we was together all through the war.

He'd cash my paycheck for me and help me in sending money home and, more important, in writing letters. The ones he sent Momma and them, and to Century and her family, he didn't mess with, but he did get me in some trouble with Belva, who already thought I'd invented World War II just to get away from her. I had told Ski enough about her, I reckon, that he knew there wasn't much between us. So one day in France on our way to Germany, he wrote some things to Belva that I don't reckon she'd ever read before. I never found out all of it, but it was enough so that she sent me a Dear John letter right quick. All things considered, I reckon I owe Ski for that one.

I'd cover for him, trying to pay him back for looking after me. If he had a date with some French girl, which he usually did despite being married, I would finish cleaning up for him and get everything ready for breakfast. A few times, I must confess, I went with him. One time, I kept Ski from a court-martial by hitting a water tower with a rock just as the lieutenant was about to catch him sleeping on guard duty.

I see these old Army movies where everybody becomes friends for life after they met in the war. Well, I haven't seen but one of my Army buddies since we all mustered out in January of 1946. The last time I saw Ski, he was fixing to get in a fight with some guy we didn't even know in Louisville, Kentucky, over something Ski had said about the fella's girlfriend. I just walked away, headed for the bus station, and by two A.M. I was on a Greyhound headed for Port Campbell. He wrote me two times, and another guy in my unit, guy named Barrera from Providence, Rhode Island, stopped by and looked me up in 1948 on the way to Florida. But Ski knew I couldn't write and didn't hardly expect a letter in return, and Barrera—I can't even remember his first name anymore—didn't have a whole lot in common with me, once the war was over.

We was luckier than most, didn't have to be right on the front lines pushing through France. Something happened toward the end, though, and maybe it affected us so much because we had let down our guard and wasn't braced for death no more. We were assigned to a mobile hospital unit, like what you see on the *M*A*S*H* TV show, and while we didn't risk our lives every day, we saw a awful lot of blood and gore. Most of us wasn't prepared for all we saw on the way to Germany, and more than one orderly or cook tried to get sent where he could meet the horror head-on instead of having it brought to him in bits and pieces. I think the farm boys, who had got their hands dirty a little more, maybe helped birth a calf or two, had it a little easier, but there was days nobody much felt like eating.

But as the fall of 1944 turned into winter, we could tell, just by how we was moving into the rising sun, that we was pushing them back toward the Rhine. Our casualties seemed like they was getting smaller and smaller, and we'd be taking that mess tent down and setting it up again so fast we didn't hardly even have time to make the meals. We was picking 'em up and settin' 'em down, as Lex used to say.

A feeling come over us that we just might beat the Germans, and we suffered more from the cold and damp than we did from incoming fire. Even the cooks had to carry M-1s, and be ready to use them, but when we crossed the Rhine and didn't meet a whole lot of Krauts where I was, we thought we must be home free. It was hard not to think about being back home, something a lot of us hadn't let ourselves do for a while.

Years after the war, when I could do it, I looked up the places we were at, because I didn't have any idea where we were at the time, just that we'd crossed the Rhine and was moving farther into Germany every day.

I had bought a cheap camera in France. Most of us had one, and the old pictures are still in the cedar chest at home. I looked at them the other day, and a lot of memories come back.

There was one of these three German girls, kind of heavy-set but good-looking, pulling this little tiny cart with wheels about two feet high. They was running away from the front, and maybe they didn't have a house to go back to, but they didn't seem real blue about it. There was pictures of long, flat fields, might of been back home in North Carolina. They grew lots of cabbage there, and we must of cooked a ton of it, none of which I ate, I can assure you. There's one picture of Lewandowski, Barrera and some guy from South Dakota—I can't even remember his name—all standing in one of them fields, all with walking sticks we'd bought from some peddler, looking like they was really something. Us and the Russians got to that part of Germany about the same time, and somewhere on the other side of Frankfurt, we started running into them. They had women with them, which we couldn't believe, although it was hard to tell that some of them was women.

The German towns that hadn't been tore up were pretty, and you could tell they really knew how to build. There was these great big square three-story brick houses with shutters and flowers in every window, so pretty you'd near-bout forget you was in a war and this was the enemy.

We took prisoners, of course. Earlier, most of them had been shipped back to places like Texas. They seemed like good enough boys, healthy-looking, athletic types that didn't seem a whole lot different from us. The ones over here wasn't much different, either. I don't recall anybody much talking about the Germans the way they did about the Japs. Fellas I knew back home would talk about them like they was the devil when they got back from the Pacific. We knew the Germans was the enemy, but we didn't despise them. Not until right at the end.

It was early April when we got to a little village several days into Germany. I took pictures of some of the road crossings so maybe somebody back home would be able to tell me where I'd been, and from that I know we was in an area that they later put behind the Iron Curtain, not that any of us that was there would likely ever want to go back to such a place, even if it wasn't.

The town itself, which wasn't no bigger than Geddie, might of been a picture postcard. Outside town, there was a camp with several rows of buildings. It had barbed wire around it, so we figured the Germans had used it to hold their own prisoners of war. It wasn't all that different from some places I'd helped guard in Texas.

The smell got to us first. We were used to the stink of death, and we'd dug our share of graves. This, though, was the rot and corruption of a dead dog left along the highway several days, but it was many times worse. We put rags over our noses as we got closer to the concrete buildings. We thought we must of happened on dead men from a battle the Germans had lost, where they'd had to leave their bodies behind in the hurry to get away.

We weren't the first Americans there, and they said that before the day was over, even Ike showed up because he couldn't believe what he'd been told. We met some other American boys coming away from the buildings, and a few of them was crying, something you didn't see much of by this time. But, like I said, our guard was down. We thought we'd seen it all already.

"I want to kill somebody!" this one GI shouted out. "I want to kill Germans till my goddamn M-1 melts!"

Some of them just had their jaws set real hard, and some just had a stare that might of been focused on something fifty miles off. One boy fell out and started puking on the ground.

We come around a corner and, up ahead, against the side

of one of the concrete buildings, we saw a window with wreaths on either side of it, and I remember thinking how funny it was that somebody hadn't took down their Christmas decorations yet. Under the wreaths and the window was a pile, about four feet high and eight feet wide, that looked for the world like a cord of firewood. But the stink would of told a dead man that this wasn't wood. It was bodies, and such bodies as none of us had ever seen before.

There must of been fifty in that one stack, more bodies than you would of thought it was possible to put in such a small pile. But these poor souls wasn't even human anymore. Most of them must of weighed less than eighty pounds, with arms you could put your forefinger and thumb around, and legs not much bigger. We found out later that the Germans had killed them all in the last forty-eight hours, just so they wouldn't live to see freedom. They were mostly Jews. One of them, piled on the top of the stack, had his head throwed back and looked out over the top of the blankets our medics had put over everything. His eyes was open, looking out at us upside down, like, "Why didn't you all get here sooner?" He was just a skeleton. His stomach was just a hole between his ribs that didn't seem to have no bottom, and he had thick black hair hanging down from the top of his skull. Most of them had been shot to death, but they would of starved anyway in a couple more days.

The saddest thing, though, were the ones still living, who looked like the dead ones, except they somehow were able to move and breathe and even talk, in German or Hebrew or something else I didn't understand. As soon as we saw them, everybody wanted to feed them, because they looked like they might fall over dead in about five minutes. Before anybody could tell us anything different, we was giving them our tins of food and our chocolate and anything else we had.

One Jew, he might of been twenty-five or sixty, just eat up with lice, ate three Hershey bars, then fell over on the ground holding his stomach and whining like a poisoned dog. Then a couple more in other parts of what was the prison yard did the same thing. And then the medics come around, calling us shitheads and telling us this food was too rich for their systems, that they couldn't digest it. Those poor souls, that had been tortured and beat and starved by the Germans for months and years, some of them was done in by chocolate bars.

We thought that maybe this death camp by this peaceful little town was the worst the Germans had to offer, that maybe this was where they sent spies or traitors or something. Then, not many miles from there, we was part of the cleanup at Buchenwald, and we saw that the first little camp was just a preview of the full-scale hell. The Germans had moved most of the Jews out just before we got there, but there was these stacks everywhere with fifty to a hundred bodies in them, and the smell was too much to be believed.

There was a chaplain with us, a Jewish fella, rabbi I reckon. He must of seen something moving in one of them piles, because he goes over and almost throws himself on all the stink and rot, and out of these bodies comes a little boy not more than ten years old. I reckon the Germans had give him up for dead. The rabbi, who had been with us all the way through France and Germany, is laughing and crying all at the same time, just overcome like the rest of us. And the little boy doesn't do anything, doesn't laugh or cry or even blink, just looks at us with the biggest, deadest eyes you ever saw.

I wonder what happened to him, how he could of lived a life after all that.

It was somewhere around there that they caught the two SS guards. I remember it was the same day I took the picture of Lewandowski and two other boys in our company standing in front of a sign that said WEIMAR and BAD BERKA, which was two towns right nearby. Lewandowski is sitting there in a squat like a hind catcher, resting on the sign, cigarette in his mouth, a match and matchbox in his hands, like he can't wait for the picture to be took so he can smoke another Lucky. That's the way I remember him.

Anyhow, on that same day, they caught some Germans trying to get some of the prisoners that was still alive out of the area. Nobody was in a real good mood. We had been coming across horror after horror until we thought horror was all we would ever be able to see again. Men, women, children, all either starved or tortured to death or just shot when they wouldn't die.

These two German SS men, probably like sergeants, was apparently trying to march a group of Jews farther east when they got cut off. Some of the prisoners told us things they had done, and all the great roaring rage that had filled us for the past few days exploded. The officers didn't try to do anything about it, either. These were great big fellas, huge muscles, one of them had a tattoo on his arm with foreign words on it. They looked scared. Several GIs made them get down on their knees, with their hands tied behind their backs, and then they let the prisoners, them that was strong enough, beat them to death with any kind of clubs they could find. It took a long time, because there wasn't many prisoners that could still lift and swing a stick. Some, even after what they had been through, wouldn't have any part of it. I reckon they couldn't believe it could be happening. Finally, some of the soldiers finished them off and we threw their bodies in a pit. And nobody ever said anything to any of us about it, one way or the other.

By May, the Germans had surrendered, and by June we was heading back west, toward a ship to carry us to the Pacific to fight the Japs. We left from Le Havre, France, on the *General Henry Taylor*. We heard about the bombs in Japan while we was still in the Atlantic. Not too long after we had went through the Panama Canal, while we was wondering how much longer the Japs could hang on, the captain came over the bullhorn and said, "Watch the shadow of this ship . . . as it turns toward New York."

It took until early '46 to get out and head home, and in some ways the last few months was the longest, just waiting and counting the days. I saw boys go AWOL and get in big trouble that had followed every order all the way across Europe.

Not me, though. I wanted to get home too bad to mess it up now. It's queer to me now to hear Georgia talk about how warm and friendly the European people are. She goes on vacation over there every chance she gets, and she can't get enough of it. To me, it was a place where God didn't live. Oh, I know God is everywhere, but maybe sometimes, in some places, He leaves for a while just to see what happens while He's gone, or maybe to test folks like He did Job. There must of been all kinds of people of France and Germany and England that looked up in a sky full of bombs and hopelessness and asked, "My God, why have you forsaken me?"

There was times, on that long trip into Germany, and especially after we knew what the Nazis had done, when it passed through me like a knife that the devil might be winning, that the whole world might be lost. It chilled me so that my bones ached all the way down to my elbows, and I would take out my Bible that I couldn't read, just to hold it.

There was a church, what they would call a cathedral, I reckon, somewhere in Germany that had been bombed all to pieces, I don't know whether by them or by us. There was a chapel there that still had a little catwalk standing along the back, even though the room and most of the insides had been blown away. I climbed up on the catwalk with my camera, aiming to take a picture looking down into the sanctuary. At the back, farthest from me, was a statue of Christ on the cross, must of been twenty feet high, between two long, high windows that had had stained glass in them before the bombs fell. The statue wasn't touched by any of the bombing around it, except that Jesus' head was gone. While I looked at it, on that cold early spring day, with the wind a-howling, a cloud passed over the sun and threw everything into deep shade, and it seemed like I could hear the devil laughing in that wind. I got down from there real fast, holding on to my Bible in my shirt pocket like it might keep Satan away.

After Buchenwald, whenever we would go into another German town, I would look at the people, just sit on a wall and stare at them for hours on end when I was off duty, trying to see what was different, what might of made them do something like they did to the Jews. And nothing I saw was much different from what you might of seen if you had sat on a bench at Dawson Autry's store in East Geddie, assuming East Geddie had just been captured by a foreign army. They was just people. They didn't have fangs or six fingers. They didn't slap their wives and children around so as I could see. They had dogs and cats, they raised gardens, they went to church on Sunday.

What it finally brought me to was slaves. I got to thinking about stories I'd heard about Aunt Mallie, how Granddaddy had took her away from most of her children, without ever thinking a thing about it, and how them and all the colored people had been chained up and shipped over from Africa, about drawings I had seen of colored families being sold separate at the slave auction in Port Campbell. And I wondered if Satan couldn't live in a place, cheek by jowl with good Christian folks, without them ever realizing he was there until it was too late.

I had known the power of Jesus, even after Lafe died, even when I was being tormented and teased because I wasn't able to learn how to read. It took Germany in 1945 to show me the power of the devil, though, and even when we was sailing out of Le Havre, I had the feeling that he might rise up out of the ground over Europe any time God turned His back for a minute. It was one of the great reliefs of my life to see the whole damned place disappear from my sight.

CHAPTER NINE

August 1

Growing up around Daddy and Uncle Lex and Aunt Connie and Grandma, without any brothers or sisters, made me feel like the Chosen Child at times, with four people so much older lavishing so much praise and attention on me all the time. Mom was a lot younger and didn't put up with as much as Daddy and the rest did.

But it also made me a little uneasy. Who's going to take

care of all these people? I'd think to my eight-year-old self. I was already intelligent enough to know that Daddy and Lex and Connie were going to take care of Grandma until she died, and that they'd done the same for Granddaddy, who died long before I was born, and that it had always been that way. I'd envy Uncle Gruff and Aunt Century for somehow escaping. Which is how I came to view our farm and East Geddie—as a place from which to escape.

It made Daddy and Mom feel bad, I know, when I'd tell them, during high school and college years, that there was nothing on earth that could make me stay in East Geddie.

"It's not *you*," I'd say once in a while when they seemed especially cut to the quick. "It's just this place."

Which was only partly true, in retrospect. It would not have been a wonderful life, coming back to East Geddie to run a farm and live among people who knew everything about me and my parents and probably my grandparents. I went back to my twenty-year high school reunion, which they held at a Holiday Inn twenty miles from the old school, for some reason. It was "dry," which didn't seem to bother anyone else. I wished that I'd brought a fifth. The worst thing was that these people, who all grew up together, seem to visit each other about as often as if they lived in separate states. There were people there who live five miles apart who seemed to be catching up on five years of news. One of the few pleasant things I could imagine about a return to East Geddie was the fantasy of getting back together with my oldest friends, after we'd raised our families and had our careers—sort of like one of those sitcom reprises where all the characters from a fifties or sixties show come back as adults under some trumped-up premise and pick up where they left off. But I don't believe it happens that way in real life. Not in East Geddie, anyhow.

The bottom line, though, truth be known, is probably that I never could face the prospect of sacrifice. This is not a solitary failing; my friends in the English department and I talk about it often. What do you do for aging parents who took care of their aging parents until the bitter end, come bedpans, Alzheimer's, nervous breakdowns (yours) or whatever? And the amazing thing is, with Daddy and Mom, they didn't even seem to mind. Even Mom, who was taking care of Daddy's mother and brother and sister, with precious little appreciation, I might add, didn't seem to bear any resentment. I would have borne quintuplets of resentment, had it been me. I see a therapist once a week now; I'd need a session a day to put up with what Mom endured. Except she didn't "endure" or even "accept." From the moment she married Daddy, she must have embraced his family as hers. It probably helped that her parents, or adopted parents, died not long after she and Daddy were married. They were much older.

After Jeff and I separated, I talked with his mother, on the phone, one time. This year, I didn't send his parents a Christmas card.

Daddy has been gypped, swindled. It isn't all my fault. I am a child of my times. We're the ones who paved the way for the Me Generation. By the time I'm old and Justin is middle-aged, children probably will be allowed to give their parents a competency test every year, and when the scores dip enough, they'll be permitted to send us to the showers, like the Jews. Sort of like SATs for the human race. Or maybe final exams.

. . .

It was shortly after Christmas of 1955 that my Uncle Gruff called and invited us to come down for a week in March. Uncle Gruff's real name is Cerrogordo. That's why he's so gruff, Daddy would tell me. He and Aunt Martha lived in Atlanta most of the time I was growing up, but they moved to the west coast of Florida for about five years before they found out early retirement didn't suit either one of them.

Daddy didn't think we ought to go, because there was so much work to do on the farm, but Mom convinced him that the Lockamys could make do for one week in March. He finally agreed, using the excuse that it would do Aunt Connie and Uncle Lex good to get away for a while, too. I'm sure Mom would have preferred for just the three of us to go, but that was out of the question.

So we packed the five of us into our green Chevrolet, Daddy and Lex in the front seat, Mom, Aunt Connie and me in the back, dressed as if we were going to church. It was the first time we'd been able to make such a trip, because Grandma had only died the year before. They had to take me out of school for a week, which I didn't mind a bit.

Thus began The Trip to Florida, capitalized because of its singular nature—my parents never went there again—and because Daddy almost killed Uncle Gruff and found a way to make money farming, a secret that had eluded our family for generations.

We drove all day and stayed at a motor court in Hardeeville, South Carolina. I remember being very discouraged because we had only gone through one state. I was eight then, and I couldn't wait to get to the state with my name, Georgia.

Then the next morning, we were in Georgia almost immediately and before we knew it, we were out of Georgia and into Florida. Daddy stopped and took my picture at the state line: one shot in front of the Florida sign, then across the road for a shot of me holding my arm out toward the Georgia sign, like, this is *my* state.

Uncle Gruff and Aunt Martha lived at a place called Jackson Island, on the Gulf of Mexico, and we had to cut across the top part of Florida to get there. A two-lane road connected the island with the mainland, across this huge savannah. It was the most lonesome place I'd ever been in my life. There were about fifty houses along the beach road, and you had to go back across the bridge to get to a grocery store. Uncle Gruff had a boat, and he'd fish for shrimp and red snapper and all kinds of seafood. I, of course, didn't like fish, so they'd fix me hamburgers or spaghetti.

The worst thing about Jackson Island was the waves. There weren't any. There was this beautiful white sand, like sugar, and there were gulls all over the place, but the Gulf around Jackson Island was like a big pond, with little ripples about six inches high. The ironic thing is that when a hurricane comes up, the waves get even higher than they do in the Atlantic, which is why Jackson Island isn't inhabited anymore.

There were also jellyfish everywhere, from little ones that just stung a little bit to big ugly ones that would raise welts. Daddy said his main memory of that trip was me standing waist deep in the Gulf, doing a complete circle every few steps to keep an eye out for jellyfish, and Uncle Gruff yelling out, "There's one, Georgia!" every once in a while, just to see me jump and scream.

There was something about standing out there in the Gulf of Mexico and looking across this flat, empty expanse that ran for a thousand miles that made me feel somehow deserted. I can't stand to be at a beach without lots of people; I'd rather go to Virginia Beach, where you can barely find space for your towel, than one of those TV beaches where some jerk strolls along the sand with his dog, no other human beings in sight, while he ponders the tragedy of receding hairline. It's strange, but mountains don't affect me that way. Jeff and I used to rent a cottage up on the west side of the Blue Ridge for a week every summer, and I couldn't get enough of just staring off into the side of a mountain from a rocking chair. But don't leave me alone at the beach.

We stayed at Jackson Island from Sunday afternoon until early Saturday morning. Uncle Gruff was a great storyteller, and everybody wanted to hear the old, old stories, ones that had been handed down like heirlooms from a widowed aunt to an older sister. Daddy knew a few, too, and between him and Gruff, I think they must have covered the whole family, all the way back to Scotland. It was the first of many tellings I can remember, and I never got tired of them.

Uncle Gruff told about how Captain McCain, my great-grandfather, came up the river from Newport, almost broke and on his way back home to Randolph County to play the prodigal returning, about how he heard about the job at Amos Geddie's sawmill while sitting in a tavern in Port Campbell and walked all the way to Geddie to talk his way into a supervisor's position. He said he'd been out west, fighting Indians or Mexicans or whatever. His family were Quakers, and he must have been the black sheep.

Daddy chimed in with the part about how the Captain

126

wooed Amos's daughter, Barbara, who was two years older than him, and no beauty to boot, and how he extorted the 320 acres of Geddie land nearest to the Blue Sandhills as a wedding present.

"And Mallie and Zebediah, too, don't forget that," Gruff said, and Daddy told us about the Captain's slaves, a couple and the one child they were allowed to take with them from the Geddie farm to the new one that was just being built, about how Mallie had to change her name to McCain, then changed it back to Geddie as soon as the war was over.

Gruff told us about the first time Captain McCain came to Geddie Presbyterian Church, when he was courting Barbara, how they told him he'd have to stand, because all the pews belonged to individual families, and how he shamed everyone by sitting on a footstool up by the choir, then putting a ten-dollar gold piece into the offering plate.

Daddy told how the captain and his son, Red John, along with the rest of the home guard, met the Union army in front of the church, supposedly to surrender, and how someone started shooting. Daddy said it was Red John, his and Gruff's daddy, but Gruff said it wasn't. Between them, they told how the Yankees chased the home guard into the sandhills and then burned everything to the ground. My favorite part was where they set the sawdust pile at the lumber yard afire and it burned and smoldered for twenty years. They called it Yankees' Revenge.

Then Aunt Connie told about the hard times after the war, when Red John's two brothers gave up their shares of the farm and went to work for their fathers-in-law, and how Red John had brought it back, borrowing for seed in the spring and using most of the harvest to pay back the loan, praying that the crops didn't fail. And Gruff told about how Red John married Faith Geddie when he was forty-nine and she was twenty-three and a widow, and about the funny names they gave their children.

They'd talk and argue and correct all night on the porch, looking out across the almost-silent waters, and I took in every word, without even knowing it at the time.

It was Thursday night that Daddy got into the argument with Uncle Gruff. Daddy almost never lost his temper, but Gruff had read something about *The Diary of Anne Frank,* which had just been made into a play, and he said that he was tired of hearing about the damn Jews, that all they'd ever done to him in Atlanta was screw him out of money, and that maybe Hitler wasn't on the wrong track after all.

Uncle Gruff had been drinking Pabst Blue Ribbon for about three hours when he said that, and I'm sure he didn't really mean it, or at least I hope he didn't, but he was always throwing around words like "nigger" and "kike" like loose change. Even in the South in 1956 he stood out, no mean feat.

Daddy didn't raise his voice.

"Don't be talking about something you don't know nothing about, Gruff," he said. He was drinking Coke and he put the glass down.

Uncle Gruff was quiet for a second or two, then he started ranting and raving about how he'd half-raised Daddy (Daddy said later all he remembered Gruff raising was hell) and how he wasn't going to take that from somebody who had to get his wife to teach him how to write his name, so what the shit did he know about politics?

Daddy told him to watch his mouth. He was a little red in the face now. But Gruff wouldn't stop. He finally made Daddy snap when he started telling us about how he used to come to Daddy's classroom at school and there would be Daddy sitting over in the corner crying because he couldn't read. Uncle Gruff was a mean drunk.

Daddy got up and went in the kitchen. He came back out with the biggest, nastiest-looking butcher knife that Uncle Gruff and Aunt Martha had taken with them from Atlanta when they retired. He walked right over to Gruff, who was trying to walk backward while still in his chair, so that he looked like one of the crabs we'd see at night on the beach, and he stuck the knife right in Gruff's face.

"If you don't shut up about the Jews, and if you don't shut up about me," Daddy told him in a strained voice so unlike his usual bass that it scared me more than the knife, "I'll cut your D head off." Daddy didn't like cursing; he might have cut Uncle Gruff's head off without ever uttering a profanity.

He backed Gruff up to the wall, where he was getting sober in a hurry. Uncle Lex tried to talk to him, and Aunt Connie took me into the hallway leading back to the bedrooms. Gruff told Daddy he was sorry, and Mom managed to walk up to him and take the knife away. Gruff sulked all the next day, but they shook hands when we left, and Gruff came to see us every year or so, even more after Aunt Martha died.

Daddy didn't show me the pictures from Germany until I was a junior in high school. Where we lived, there was nothing but white Anglo-Saxon Protestants in the high school. The blacks and Indians went to their own schools, and all the Jews lived in town. I guess they burned the Catholics at the stake or something.

It's painful for me to look back and see the way we were, but all the I'm-sorry's in the world won't make it any different.

They had integrated the schools that year, fall of 1965, and nobody—at least, nobody white—was very happy about it. Even Daddy grumbled about the federal government trying to tell us what to do, and Mom said it would be the end of the state education system. Even then, whites were pulling their kids out of schools all over and starting their own segregation academies.

The first two years, it was voluntary. There were six blacks in the junior class, another seven in the sophomore class and a dozen freshmen. Their lives must have been total hell. Nobody actually did serious bodily harm to any of them, just called them niggers about two trillion times, and painted it on their lockers, and laughed at their accents—which weren't much if any worse than ours, probably—and in general tried to make them commit suicide.

One of them did. Latricia Wonsley was her name. She went home after her biology teacher ridiculed her for "axing" for something and the whole class joined in, reducing her to tears. She went home, got a chair from the kitchen table, stood on it with a piece of clothesline she'd cut, tied it around her neck and secured it to a light fixture, kicked the chair away and hanged herself right there in the living room. They said she had been an A student at her old school, Carver High, and her parents expected her to show the white kids at Geddie High what a smart black girl could do when she had the chance. She obviously never had the chance. A month before she killed herself, someone had smeared her locker door, which was right next to mine, with Crisco, a crude allusion to the Royal Crown Pomade black people used in those days when they still so desperately seemed to need to be white. A couple of white boys allegedly exposed themselves to her in an empty classroom, and nobody was ever punished. There were different books, different methods, and nobody ever tried to help Latricia Wonsley figure them out.

The day after it happened, it was all over school, of course, and Mike Draughon told Bonnie Cain and me that it was the sight of Ernest Naylor's penis—except he didn't say penis, of course—that drove her to it. We were a very clever, witty crowd.

When I got home that day—it was sometime after Christmas and before spring planting—Daddy was inside, sitting by the oil heater eating parched peanuts. It was just before we moved into Grandma's old house, after Lex and Connie died.

"Nigger girl killed herself last night," I said, swelled in the importance of imparting grownup news.

He stopped shelling peanuts and asked me who she was. I told him Latricia Wonsley. He said that her mother used to do laundry for us, and that he'd known her daddy since before the war. Daddy knew everybody in Geddie, East Geddie and Old Geddie back then.

"We ought to fix something and take it down there," he said, thinking a coconut pie or a cake or something. People have been known to gain five pounds at a loved one's funeral in the Geddies.

I told him I didn't think that was a very good idea, because the Wonsleys, whoever they were, probably hated white people.

He asked me how come, and I told him about some of the "jokes" that my more mean-spirited classmates, with the full consent and approval of the silent majority, had played on Latricia (leaving out the part where she was exposed to Ernest Naylor's not-so-private parts, of course).

Daddy and Mom had heard me tell some of the stories at supper, and if they didn't laugh out loud, they seemed to accept it as just part of high school pranks. Making life hard for black people was the official pastime of Scots County, after all.

"So you think she killed herself because you all were so mean to her?" he asked me. I wasn't ready to accept responsibility for Latricia Wonsley's suicide, and I told him so. Told him that she apparently couldn't take a joke very well.

He got up and threw the peanut shells and newspaper he'd held in his lap into the trash, then went into his and Mom's bedroom. He was gone about five minutes, and I thought we were through talking about Latricia Wonsley. I got myself a Pepsi out of the refrigerator and was sitting on the couch when he came back in with a handful of photographs.

"I got something I want to show you," he said. "It's some pictures I took when I was in the Army, during the war."

He'd never shown me those pictures, and he'd never talked about the war other than to say he was a cook, which didn't appear to be the kind of thing you'd use for bragging material in the neighborhood.

What really got to him, Daddy said after he'd showed me the pictures of the Jews, was the German people. I saw what he intended for me to see in the pictures of them: There was relief, of course, there was obsequiousness, there was a certain haughtiness. Nowhere, though, was there any shame. And, like Daddy said, the Germans might as well have been us. They had little dogs and gardens and wore hats and went to school.

Daddy took the pictures from me and put his hairy, freckled hand on mine.

"When you don't treat folks like human beings," he said, "something terrible can happen. Let's us don't be like that."

This was the beginning of my liberal education, coming from a Southern farmer who still called (and still calls) blacks "colored people." It would be two more years, in my freshman year at UNC–G, before another teacher would broach this still-delicate matter of Southern whites treating blacks like garbage. And within four years, I was exercising the college student's God-given right to assume omniscience and was lecturing Daddy on the atrocities of the South. He handled it as he did most things, with grace.

I would like to say that a veil was lifted from my eyes and that I went and sinned no more after Daddy showed me his war pictures. But is there a sixteen-year-old who isn't mainly powered by the force of peer pressure? I certainly wasn't strong enough to rebel against it. We still either laughed at black kids or acted as if they didn't exist. It was more like I'd still do and say these hateful things, but later I would think about what I did and feel guilty. It took years for my guilt reflexes to get quick enough to kick in *before* I did a spiteful thing to another person.

And Daddy and Mom weren't saints. They still felt as if the feds were bringing back Reconstruction, but they were able to separate the cause from the effect, so that they didn't, as lots of my friends' parents did, treat black children like the chosen instruments of the Evil Empire in Washington.

It probably helped Mom that she had to spend a summer school at Carver. She had never been in a black high school before, but the summer before my senior year, she was persuaded to teach a course there in remedial English to help some of the kids make the transition to the white world.

She would come home at first angry, then sorrowful, about conditions at the school, how the state had let it fall into such disrepair that nothing much could save it. Mom had grown up in the building industry, and she knew crappy construction when she saw it. But it didn't stop there. She saw kids having to share books. She saw the poor food— even by school lunchroom standards—they were getting. She wrote the superintendent a letter spelling it out, chapter and verse, and she was not asked to teach summer school again. When white kids started getting bused to Carver, though, they tore the damn thing down and built Sandy Heath High, for all races, creeds and colors, within another school year.

It was on the way back from Uncle Gruff and Aunt Martha's that Daddy hit on his big idea. The farm was not doing all that well; it took a lot of people to work 320 acres the right way. Daddy always said the farm was just big enough to be dangerous. It wasn't one of those farms in the Midwest where you can't see from one end to the other, and it wasn't a manageable little eighty-acre tract. Uncle Lex was over sixty, Daddy had just turned fifty and Rennie's children seemed to want to leave home as soon as they got old enough to get a job. I can't imagine why they didn't want to work for Daddy and Uncle Lex for nothing.

Cropping tobacco is what you'd call labor intensive. It became more and more of a problem for farmers around here in the sixties and seventies, when federal programs finally gave poor people an alternative to chopping cotton and cropping tobacco for seventy-five cents an hour and all the watermelon they could eat. You won't find many fans of Uncle Sam around Geddie, unless he wants them to send their sons halfway across the planet to get their legs blown off in somebody else's war, but, as far as I'm concerned, they brought it on themselves. They could have integrated the schools themselves, and not made such a bloody mess of it. They could have taken care of their own poor, set up programs to teach people how to do useful, productive things and then pay them a living wage.

The farmers would sit around the store and complain about how nobody wanted to work anymore, but you couldn't have gotten one of them to pay those people enough to live on if you'd put a gun to their heads. It made them mad that the feds were stealing their slave labor away. Daddy used to tell me about one man, Loftus Bedsole, who had a farm between McNeil and Cool Spring. Loftus Bedsole hated the government so much that he wouldn't drive on U.S. highways. He drove to Richmond one time to visit his sister and her husband, and he took nothing but state and local roads all the way up. It was a nine-hour drive, and when he got there, he had to call them to come and get him. They lived on a U.S. highway.

Anyhow, when we were leaving Uncle Gruff's, he gave us

a quicker route back home. We wound up on 301, which took us across a larger, uglier stretch of Georgia. Before we got to the South Carolina line, Daddy was threatening to rename me Kansas or Connecticut or Wisconsin, anything but Georgia.

A few miles after we crossed the Savannah River into South Carolina, we started seeing signs that said PICK YOUR OWN STRAWBERRIES.

Since it was March, there wasn't anything to pick, but the farmer didn't want to go to the trouble of taking his signs down, I guess. It was getting late in the afternoon, and Aunt Connie was becoming a little anxious to find a place to stay for the night, but Daddy was intrigued by just about anything concerning farming, and he followed the signs. We turned left down a two-lane county road, followed it about two miles, then turned left at another strawberry sign and went up a dirt road that dead-ended at a big farmhouse.

There were strawberry beds all around the house and room for parking alongside it. A big spitz tried to chew our tires off, and we had just about decided to turn around and leave when a man came out of the house and shooed the dog away.

Daddy got out and introduced himself, and he and Uncle Lex and the man went off talking farming. The man's wife, and I never did learn either one of their names, invited Mom and Aunt Connie and me inside for iced tea.

The rest of the way back, including half the night in the tourist park where we stayed, Daddy and Uncle Lex talked about strawberries. Daddy said the soil along the back side of their property would be perfect for them, but Uncle Lex wasn't sure, and he wasn't eager to get into something that would require a loan and would take a couple of years to get going. He was eleven years older than Daddy and said he had nightmares about having to spend his old age in the poor-house. By the time we got back to East Geddie, though, Daddy had talked him into going into the pick-your-own-strawberries business, and had talked Mom and Aunt Connie and me into it, too.

Daddy and Uncle Lex wound up leasing several acres from the McDaniels, who were just about out of farming by that time, anyhow, and pieced that together with some of the swamp land they already owned. They eventually did well enough off strawberries that they were able to buy twenty acres from the McDaniels.

Daddy and Rennie and Uncle Lex and one of Rennie's boys who wasn't old enough to leave home yet built a big shed off the Ammon Road and ran a dirt road in from that side. Daddy said he didn't want a bunch of strangers all the time coming up our road and parking in our driveway. They couldn't plant strawberries until the next March, by which time they'd had to take out a mortgage on the farm to pay for an irrigation system and all the fertilizer and plastic sheeting that Daddy said they'd have to put under the plants. This was something he said he'd read about in the *Progressive Farmer,* something he said they could do to improve on the operation we'd seen in South Carolina. Taking out a mort-gage on the farm worried Uncle Lex almost to death.

The farmers around Geddie and East Geddie thought Daddy had lost his mind. The last change most of them had made was to switch to tobacco sometime after World War

I. They'd kid him, during the two years it took to get the business going, asking him when he was going to bring them some strawberries.

"You'll have to pay for them, and you'll have to pick them," he'd say. It never bothered Daddy to go against the grain, or the tobacco. It probably bothered me more. Kids whose parents would talk about the crazy McCains and their strawberries would call me "Strawberry," but Daddy told me not to worry, that those strawberries would pay my way through college.

He was right, and so was his timing. They were just getting ready to open the interstate that runs a little east of the river at Port Campbell, not more than five miles from East Geddie. Daddy and Uncle Lex paid for space on a couple of billboards, driving Uncle Lex into even deeper depression, I'm sure, as he saw more money flying out the window. But Daddy knew that half the East Coast would come through on the interstate, and if he could just get one in a thousand to take a short side trip, they'd have all the business they needed.

Which is just what happened. The idea of picking your own strawberries was fairly new at the time, and Daddy picked up one good idea from the man in South Carolina: He advertised that you could eat all you wanted while you picked. Daddy would charge enough to make up for all a starving person could possibly eat. And everybody over-picked. They figured they'd gone to the trouble to find the place (Daddy was smart enough not to mention our town's name, so we avoided the usual confusion that hits when people go east from Geddie and can't find East Geddie), so they ought to pick plenty. I'm sure trash cans in rest stops all the way from Maine to Florida were full of McCain strawberries. They probably still are. There's a sucker passing by every minute on the interstate.

People from Port Campbell and the Geddies would come and pick, too, and many people would just slip in at night and pick for free, which never bothered Daddy very much.

"If they need food that bad," he'd say, "let them pick."

All through my high school years, I'd spend afternoons in May and into June out there weighing strawberries and ringing up sales. Daddy or Rennie would load the pickers on a flatbed wagon hitched to a tractor and tow them out to the parts of the patch that were ready to pick. Uncle Lex and Aunt Connie and Mom all pitched in, and they'd have to hire lots of extra help to cut the runners in the fall and pick off the flowers in the early spring. But Daddy was right. The soil there, on the edge of the Blue Sandhills, was perfect for strawberries. They branched out into blueberries and blackberries later, so that there was always something to pick in warm weather, it seemed.

Even while we were starting to rake in the money off Daddy's idea, I didn't much like the berry business. When we had tobacco, I could avoid doing much farm work, other than picking peas and beans and shelling them, and helping Mom with the canning. Daddy didn't want his little girl to get her hands all grimy with tobacco juice and be around people that would bite tobacco worms in half for a quarter. But the strawberries were different. It was more meeting people than manual labor, from my end, and it didn't hurt sales, as I got a little older, to have a cute girl at the counter. But I was never what they call smart around here, meaning I never was too crazy about working from sunrise to sunset.

I'd take a book with me and read every second somebody wasn't waddling up with twenty pounds of strawberries they didn't need.

By high school, it really started to grate on me that I was stuck around that shed when my friends were going to the lake or the beach. Looking back, I had it pretty soft, but I didn't feel that way then.

CHAPTER TEN

August 8

The war cleansed my spirit, for a spell.

All the dying, big and little, made what had happened with Lafe seem like it was somehow smaller, less awful. At some time in Germany, toward the end, I quit talking to Lafe's ghost, forgot I'd ever met Angora Bosolet.

Now, back home in 1946 with February going fast into March and the land waiting to be led into spring, it seemed almost like I was born again. It wasn't a religious thing, although there wasn't a day in the war I didn't pray, first for my own selfish hide, then for the people we saw, then for the whole sorry world. It was more like I really was a new person with a new life in front of me. Momma had failed a lot, was a lot more feeble at seventy-six than she had been at seventy-two, and Lex and Connie seemed like they depended on me to get things going again.

The farm was doing right poorly. There wasn't enough help during the war, but the real problem was that Lex wasn't getting any younger, and he had been spending more and more time working at the lumber yard and less time looking after the farm, which he mostly left to Rennie's family. Since Rennie and his folks wasn't hardly making enough off sharecropping to buy food, they wasn't exactly killing themselves to keep things up.

So I come home to a house with full electricity, indoor plumbing and a brand-new Chevrolet in the carhouse, because times was good at the lumber yard, and to a farm that was drying up on one end and drowning on the other. They had let the crop ditch get all clogged with weeds so that the near fields wasn't getting enough water. The swamp, on the other hand, was only being half farmed, partly because it was so wet, without the crop ditch to drain some of the water off, partly because Rennie's folks didn't have the time or inclination to do all that ought to of been done.

They said I'd changed some, and I reckon they were right. I still couldn't read and write, but there was this feeling that if I'd got through four years of World War II, I must not be a complete idiot.

I throwed myself back into the farm, but it was out of love

of the land instead of needing a place to hide. We was too late to get back the rest of the swamp land for that year, but we did work like the devil and got the crop ditch bush-axed and drug so water flowed to the near fields again. And while Lex and Connie had took care of all the modern conveniences for the inside of the house, they'd pretty much let the outside go to hell, so there was a lot of painting and roofing going on that spring. These old pine farmhouses just drink paint; we must of put three coats on before it looked right. But that was okay by me; I was just glad to be home.

I went back to my place in the choir, and they said they sure had missed me. Belva was talking to me, but we weren't likely to get back together, which was okay, too. Everything seemed like it was a little bit smaller now, but that was the way I wanted it. The world didn't ever have to get no bigger than East Geddie again, far as I was concerned.

There was new faces. Folks had moved in to work at the mill when the men went off to war, and there was lots of people hanging around the store and going to church that I didn't know. There was others that had changed so much that I didn't know them, either, although I'd been around them most all of my life. Sara Blue was one. And even knowing what I knew later, I wouldn't of done anything different.

She was eighteen when I joined the Army, near-bout twenty-three when I got back. I barely remembered a skinny, dark-haired girl with eyes like new pennies that didn't seem to have no respect for her elders. She was always sitting toward the back of the church, usually with a girlfriend or two, passing notes and dropping their heads down to hold in their giggles.

She was the daughter of Miss Annie Belle and Mr. Hector

Blue. Mr. Hector had been running the plywood plant over at McNeil for the Godwins for as long as I could remember. Him and Miss Annie had adopted Sara, and they give her just about anything she wanted. Folks said she was spoiled rotten as a young-un.

She'd been gone, too, the first college girl from around here. The Blues sent her to Women's College in Greensboro in 1938, although her and her folks told me it like to of killed them to let her go. She'd graduated from high school at fifteen and was back here teaching at nineteen. I don't reckon I'd seen her more than a few times since 1938.

She told me later that even though nobody could of been better to her than the Blues, she had always felt like a orphan, somehow. She said it made it easier to leave home. So I asked her why she come back to East Geddie. So I could have you, she said.

By the time I got back home in 1946, she was a grown woman, singing in the choir instead of cutting up on the back row. She was a English teacher at Geddie School. At the first choir practice I went to, she introduced herself and called me Mr. McCain, which made me feel right old. I was near-bout forty then.

I was attracted to her, without really knowing it at first. She was still a young-un in my mind, but there was something that struck a chord, that made me want to be with her. I tried to put the feeling aside, because it was just silly, a old farmer that couldn't even read and write going after a young schoolteacher with four years of college. I had only been with Rose and a few French whores in my whole life and, until

Sara, I figured that that might be it. Me and Lex and Connie and Momma looking after each other.

Even after four years in the Army, I was a little touchy about not being able to read. Every time the choir learned a new hymn, it was agony for me, because I'd have to learn it all by heart, somehow, just kind of humming along and listening the first couple of times we went over it. Good thing for me we didn't change songs much.

But while I was gone, they had picked up a couple that was second nature to everybody else and Greek to me. It shamed me to have to stumble like that in front of the choir, but especially in front of Sara. At about the third choir practice, I reckon, she started standing next to me, managed to change places with Harwood Bryant, which suited me, because she smelled a lot better than Harwood, who dipped snuff. She would read the verses we was to sing, usually 1, 2 and 4, to me beforehand, without making a big deal out of it, and it helped me learn it faster. I could remember, even if I couldn't read.

It was after Easter and just before my fortieth birthday that I come to realize that she might see me as something other than a wore-out old bachelor.

We had choir practice on Wednesday nights, and I've got to confess that I did fix myself up a little more than I did before the war. I'd shave, for the second time that day, wash real good, since I had just got in from the fields, and put on a clean pair of pants and a shirt that Connie pressed for me.

"Littlejohn," she'd say, "I can't believe you're a bachelor. If I wasn't your sister, I'd marry you myself." She could still make me blush.

So this Wednesday in late April, we'd just finished for the evening and was walking toward the front door when Sara, who had been telling me something about the garden she had at her folks' house, started going through her pocketbook kind of frantic.

She put her right hand on my left arm, just above the elbow. I couldn't believe how warm and nice it felt. It was the first time she'd ever touched me.

"Mr. McCain," she said, the edge of a smile showing, "I believe I have lost my car keys. I'm afraid I might have locked them in the car."

Her daddy's Ford was parked right next to Lex's Chevrolet. We was the last ones out of the church and closed the door—nobody had to lock up churches back then. I walked with her to the Ford, and, sure enough, there was the keys locked up inside, right on the dash.

"I can't believe I did that," she said. "Damn!" Right there in the church yard. I'd never heard a woman cuss at church before. I could smell the honeysuckle that was just coming out across the Old Geddie Road. I told her not to worry.

Lex had some wire in the boot of his car, and I cut a piece off with the pliers from his toolbox that he carried back there, too. I made a loop and worked the wire between the rubber and the top of the glass enough to drop it down on the lock. It was like trying to pick up the watch with the steam shovel at the county fair. Finally, on the fourth try, I hooked the loop around the lock and pulled it up.

"You certainly are handy, Mr. McCain," she said after she thanked me. I was standing by the front door as she opened it, and stepped to one side. Then she reached up and kissed me, right on the lips. She was kind of short, five foot three, so she had to put one of her warm hands behind my neck and kind of draw me down to her.

"Why don't you just call me Littlejohn?" I said, my voice kind of hoarse.

"I've been wanting to do that for three months," she said, and I hoped she meant kiss me, not call me Littlejohn. We kissed each other again, slower this time. If she had told me she wanted me to take Lex's car and drive it off Meade's Landing into the Campbell River, I would of done it, no questions asked.

"You know," she said, "Daddy's getting pretty tired of my taking his car every Wednesday night. He says he and Momma might have somewhere they want to go. Would you mind picking me up on Wednesdays from here on out?"

I was in a daze. As I tried to walk around to the driver's side of the Chevy, I slipped in the wet grass and like to of broke my leg. I must of made one romantic sight pulling myself up with the back fender of Lex's car. I didn't look over to see if Sara was watching me, but she couldn't hardly of missed that. Fool, I was saying to myself. Fool, fool, fool.

On Sunday, I was eat up with anticipation, waiting to see her and talk to her again. In the choir room before the sermon, she only give me a smile that didn't seem like it meant anything, and I wondered if she'd changed her mind, or if I had dreamed it all. Would I make a bigger ass of myself than I already had by showing up at Mr. Hector Blue's house on Wednesday?

But after the service, as we was leaving the room, I felt that hand on my elbow and smelled that perfume.

"Don't forget me now, on Wednesday, Littlejohn."

So we started going to choir practice together, which was not lost for a minute on the other choir members, including Belva's cousin Lizzie. From the way some people at my church acted, you would of thought we had committed adultery in the pulpit. I know folks around here that have spent their whole lives worrying about what everybody else at church will think if they do such-and-such. About the only time I let what other people thought get in my way was with Rose. If I paid any mind to what some of the folks around here thought, I'd of been in Dix Hill a long time ago. The people I have known all my life, grown up and gone to school and church with and hung around the store with, they're good folks, but they can be right narrow-minded.

We would go back to Sara's daddy's and talk out on the porch until eleven o'clock sometimes. She would ask me all about the war, about the people in Europe, and she would tell me how silly and worthless she felt staying back here when everybody was getting killed and all. She said she tried to join the WACs in 1942, that if somebody that knew Mr. Hector hadn't called him from the enlistment office, she would of.

She said she was fixing to move to her own place, that Mr. Godwin that owned the lumber yard and plywood plant had a house he would rent her, and that she couldn't live with her momma and daddy all her life. I thought of Connie and Lex.

It was June before her folks would invite us inside and offer us some coffee, and neither them nor Momma was too happy about us getting serious.

"When she's forty-three, you'll be sixty," Momma would say, which made no sense to me. "And how are you all going to live here? This place is just right for four people. It'd be too little for five.''

I didn't trouble to mention that we used to have eight of us here, or that at one time or another during the Depression, we'd had three different cousins or uncles living here, including Cousin Livonia, who had a baby with her. I didn't bother to mention that Momma was twenty-six years younger than Daddy. I just did what I knew was the best thing. No sense arguing with family and getting everybody stirred up.

What Mr. Hector and Miss Annie was telling Sara, I don't know, but it got back to me that they wasn't exactly dancing in the front yard. I reckon they might of asked Sara how she could be sent to college, get a good education, then come back and hook up with a dirt farmer that couldn't even spell ''cat.'' Well, she was working on that, too. Sara always had a plan.

She knew right off, of course, that I was illiterate. That was no big secret around here, but it wasn't quite the problem it would be today. You could manage to vote if you couldn't read, long as you was white, and they'd read you the questions on the driving test so you could get your license if you had sense enough to learn them by heart. Not being able to read was just something I took for granted, like Daddy having one leg or Jeff Bullock being blind.

We had been courting for three months, Wednesdays and Sundays, when she made her first move to do something about the problem, or at least try.

''Littlejohn,'' she said one night when we was sitting on a bench at McNeil Park, looking across the river at the fireflies and listening to the music coming up from the band on Scots Landing, down beneath us, "I'd like for you to do something for me. Will you promise?"

I reckon I would of promised anything, and I did.

"I want you to take a little test for me," she said.

I told her tests was for young-uns in school, but she kept on, reminding me that I'd promised. She said she'd give me the test the next time we met, four days from then on Sunday.

That Sunday night, Sara come to dinner at Momma's. Lex and Connie was as nice as could be, and Momma was tolerable. She might cut a shine about me and Sara when it was just me, but she knew better than to insult Sara. Then after supper, me and Sara went out on the back porch. She asked me to cut on the porch light, and she took out a couple of pieces of paper. One of them had letters wrote on it, big block letters like they have in grade school, which brought back nothing but bad memories.

"What I want you to do," she said, "is to copy what's on this sheet of paper on this clean one here. Just like you see it."

I didn't want to. Nobody wants to look like a fool in front of his girl. What finally persuaded me, I'm ashamed to say, is that she leaned over next to me and whispered in my ear what she would do for me if I would do this for her.

"And you know I keep my promises," she said.

What she had wrote on the paper was that sentence they give you on typing tests: NOW IS THE TIME FOR ALL GOOD MEN TO COME TO THE AID OF THEIR COUNTRY. She kept my version of it and showed it to me years later. ZOM IS EHT TIW

Littlejohn

EOR RL GOD MEM OT COV DT HEL VIO OE HTR ONTY, except some of the letters weren't even right side up and forward.

Sara looked at what I had took fifteen minutes to write. She didn't laugh, and she didn't frown like maybe her folks was right after all. Sara just looked up, real earnest, and said, "Honey, how would you like to be able to read and write?"

First, we spent several nights just working on the letters. But it wasn't like she'd write them up on the board and I'd try to copy them off. She had me make like I was writing all the letters, capital and small, all the way through the alphabet, except she had me do the motions with my whole arms. We did that for three nights, two hours each. Then, a little bit at a time, she worked me down to where I was just using my right hand to make the motions, so I could wake up in the middle of a sound sleep and make a capital "V" or a little "r" without thinking a-tall.

After a while, she'd have me do the letters without anything wrote down to go from. Then she had me writing whole little words, then bigger words. I'd repeat the letters as she said them, and then make all the motions that made up each letter. Like if she said "cat," I'd make motions like a old tomcat walking, with my fingers. After doing that a few times, I felt like my brain knew what the word "cat" looked like.

Then she'd make me write all the letters of a word without even seeing the word. She used lined school paper so I'd know where to stop each line of every letter. After a spell, she'd make me do it with plain paper. And she had me say the letters while I wrote them.

When we got to sentences, she'd make me act out the

whole thing, then write it out a letter and then a word at a time. I had to show her the meaning of every single word while I wrote them.

Next, she read to me, just stories for young-uns. She would read every sentence to me, twice in my left ear, twice in my right ear, and then twice behind me. She said she was teaching me to listen, something I thought I was already doing a right good job of. Then she would have me read the same sentence. I was supposed to act out every word of it, and it took us months just to get through a few little Bible stories for children. But when she was finished, I could at least do a passable job of reading and writing.

Two things was working in my favor.

One was what Sara called ego, meaning I didn't get my feelings hurt easy. Everybody in both families and two thirds of Geddie and East Geddie knew that Littlejohn McCain was trying to learn how to read and write, like some schoolboy, and I reckon we could of made a fortune by charging admission to watch me play-act them words and sentences. In a little town like this, without much going on but work, something like me trying to learn to read and write was more entertainment than a fire. But it bothered Sara more than it did me. They'd tease her right much at school and at church about keeping me after class and such nonsense as that, and that beautiful dark complexion of hers would get even darker, and her brown eyes would look like fire. I told her not to let it bother her, because then the folks that was picking at us would of won.

The other thing was patience. When I try to explain it, it sounds like something we did in a few weeks. Truth is, we'd been married and had Georgia before I got so I could read a whole book, even a young-un's book, on my own. Georgia once told me how she thought, when she was a little girl, that all mommas worked with the daddies and children on their reading, although she couldn't figure what school it was I went to every day in my overalls.

But there's something about walking behind a kiss-fired mule several hours and a few miles every day, or spending hour after hour clearing out a ditch or harvesting corn, and knowing it'll all have to be done over and over again, or you'll starve, that makes you right calm and patient, although there's been plenty of impatient farmers, I reckon. I'm just not sure how good a farmer they could of been. But, like I told Sara, I was made for the long haul. Must be about half mule myself. I can work a field all day long, summer or winter, or I can sit on that back porch and look out across the woods for half a day if there's nothing to do, just thinking.

Nobody seems like they can wait anymore. Jenny was telling me about her neighbor's boy the other day. His daddy, Tom McNeil that I went to school with's son, bought the boy a new car when he was sixteen, because he just had to have one. Then he paid his way to Carolina, where he changed his major three times and never did graduate. Him and his girlfriend got married when he was twenty-two and she was nineteen, and Jenny says that his daddy has had to get him out of trouble with charge cards at least twice that she knows of because if they go out to Circuit City and see something they just have to have right now, they'll just whip out the little plastic card like it was magic. Now the boy's twenty-five and his daddy is cosigning a loan for them to buy a house, and the boy has quit his job as a draftsman to go into real estate, which he don't know the first thing about, because he reckons he can get rich quick.

I don't know. Maybe if I was growing up now, I'd be impatient, too. It was easy being patient back then. Lots of practice.

By the summer of 1946, me and Sara knew we were going to get married. We made it official in August and set the wedding for November. Nobody tried real hard to talk us out of it, although the Blues weren't doing somersaults. Everybody knew how useless it was to try and change Sara's mind once it was made up, and I reckon they figured I was right contrary, too.

What I wanted, although I hadn't told Momma or Lex or Connie yet, was a house for just me and Sara. We talked about moving into her place that she was renting, but like I told her, farming was my job and I had to be right next to the farm. Finally, I talked it over with Lex, and he agreed to let me have the little patch of land next to Momma's, between her house and the highway. It wasn't his to give, but Momma let him make all the decisions by this time. Then I talked with Mr. Hector about lumber and cinder blocks and all the other building material, and he threw in most of it as a wedding present. Sara and me paid cash for the rest. So that fall, after the tobacco had gone to market and in between cutting ditch bank and hog killing and pulling the last of the corn, we started building me and Sara a house.

It like to of killed Momma. You would of thought we was going to the moon. All of a sudden, that house that would of been too small for five people would seem too empty and lonesome with just three. I reckon four was the only number

Momma could abide with anymore. I knew she'd get over it, though, so me and Sara just rode out the storm.

We got married on November 17, 1946, with Lex as my best man and Jack Tatum and Paul Draughon as ushers. Sara's daddy give her away, of course. Two of her friends from Greensboro, who were teaching now, too, in Sanford and Charlotte, and Bonnie Cain, her best friend from high school, was her bridesmaids. When I look back at the pictures now, I look like a fella going to the electric chair, which is peculiar, because I know it was the happiest day of my whole life.

That first winter, we lived at Momma's, staying in the same bedroom I had all my life, the one I had shared with Lafe and then had to live in alone after he died. It was a room where bad memories was as close as the place on the wall behind the headboard where Lafe had carved both our initials. For years, I just come to that room after supper and went to sleep, then got up in the morning, put on my clothes before I had hardly even opened my eyes, and went back to work. Now, I noticed things. There was the one old pair of pants hanging up in the back of the closet, where Momma never went anymore, that was the only piece of clothes of Lafe's that was still here. After he died, when I couldn't bear to even think about Lafe, Momma made me wear his clothes when mine wore out, said there weren't any sense in wasting money on new clothes when there was perfectly good ones right there in the closet. There was a stack of old newspapers and magazines back in the plunder room that you got to by pulling a piece of my bedroom wall out. It was stuff that Lafe had collected, mostly about World War I, with a clipping from the *Port Campbell Post* about the time Babe Ruth and the

Yankees come to town. There was a big picture with that one, of the whole ball field with the crowd near-bout falling onto the field. Back behind first base, Lafe had drawed a circle around the tree where me and him and Leonidas McNeil had sat, with a arrow pointing to it and some writing above it. Sara read it to me, because I still couldn't read too good:

"My brother Littlejohn and Leonidas McNeil and I at the baseball game between the Yankees and the Port Campbell Grays."

There was too many memories in that room. When we moved out after the house was done in May of 1947, the only thing I took was Lafe's senior yearbook. I wish to God I hadn't took anything.

Me and Lex and the Tatums and the Williamses and some of the Blues' younger kin built Sara's and my house. It wasn't real big, and since it was built out in the middle of a field, it didn't have no shade for a long time. We built a big bedroom for us, a little one for the baby that was on the way, a kitchen where we ate, a living room and a screened-in porch facing east, which is where we just about lived the first few summers. We built on a bigger living room later and made the first one into a den, and we built a little sewing room for Sara, where she could go when she wanted to read or grade papers. She never did learn how to sew.

Momma would come over about twice a day for one thing or another, and she had a perfectly good chinaberry tree cut down from the west side of her house, claiming that she was afraid that the old tree would fall down in a hurricane. It give her a clear view of our porch until Sara bought some floor-length shades. Momma didn't like that too much, but Sara humored her for the most part.

The first year and a half we was married, I was just a young-un in a candy store. I don't mean sex, or at least not just sex. It was more like I was just discovering the world. There was just so much that wasn't there before the war. I was just getting so I could read; I'd go for the newspaper every day like it was manna from heaven, reading the funnies first, then going to the sports pages, then trying to make out the local news and the national news. Sara helped me with the big words. She had saved her teacher's salary and bought us a brand-new car, a green Plymouth two-door, and on Saturday afternoons, we'd just go out driving sometimes. We'd go up to Raleigh, or over to Chapel Hill. One day, when we was still living at Momma's, we went to White Oak Beach without telling anybody. It was the first time I'd been there since we used to take the excursion train when we was teen-agers. The beach wasn't so run-down then, and Sara and me had a good time. We rode on the Ferris wheel, which like to of scared me to death, and the roller coaster, which was worse. We hadn't even thought to buy bathing suits, so we took off our shoes and waded along the edge of the ocean, running up the sand when the waves come in. We ate cotton candy and we felt like we was the Rockefellers. We didn't get back until after midnight, mostly because I had to change a tire over east of Cool Spring, and when we pulled into the driveway, we saw that every light at Momma's was on. It turned out that they got to missing us about nine o'clock and figured there was no sensible reason for us to be gone that long without telling anybody, so they had the sheriff looking for us.

"Mrs. McCain," Sara told her after we'd rushed in, scared that she'd died or something, "you're going to lose an awful lot of sleep trying to keep up with us."

We had a tractor by now and a little more money, and farming weren't as rough as it had been, although it didn't pay very good. But I did have more time to spend with Sara, which was good, especially after Georgia was born. I'd come back for dinner and stay for three hours sometimes. She'd took some home-ec courses at Women's College, and she was a good cook but in a different way from Momma or Connie. She'd fix things I never ate before, like spaghetti and meatballs or chicken with all kinds of sauces that were so good that you'd sop it up with the biscuits so you didn't waste none of it. I used to tease Sara about making a chicken last two weeks like that, but she sure was a good cook.

She said she had studied learning problems like mine at college, and that she had a professor that had all kinds of new ideas on how to teach people to read. Said it would shock people to know how many folks there was that had the same problem I did and just hid it as best they could, all their lives. She used to kid me that the reason she pretended to fall in love with me was so she could use me as a guinea pig. I know this: She could spot it a mile away, and there was more than one student that come into her tenth-grade English class at the high school not being able to read that was able by the time they graduated. She said she was always amazed that they could get that far, but it didn't amaze me. If you was able to put up with enough abuse, they'd finally just let you move on up the ladder.

Littlejohn

When I get upset about something, or get in a hurry, I still mess up. I won't likely ever win any spelling bees, and I try to keep my notes short and sweet. I don't send Christmas cards, now that Sara's gone. And it took me a year to finish *Huckleberry Finn,* when I was forty-two. But in the summer of 1947, with me and Sara sitting in our new house and the baby on the way, there wasn't nothing on God's earth that I wanted for. I had it all.

We lived in that little house for twenty-one years, until Momma and then Lex and Connie died and Georgia was a junior at Women's College, which by now even had a few boys at it. I never wanted to move back into the old house, but Sara had some ideas that she'd been sitting on since she first saw the place, and she talked me into moving everything we owned fifty yards away, to Momma's, and we rented out our place.

We'd saved right much, between her salary and the farm, especially with the berry business doing better all the time, and it didn't cost that much to send Georgia to a state school. Anyway, we had rent money coming in, too, from white-trash families, one of which eventually burnt the house down. So we were able to put in baseboard heat and a new kitchen, have the tile took up and the old oak floors stripped and redone so they probably looked better than they did when my granddaddy and them built the place. We put jacks under the floor in places where the termites had done the most damage, and it creaks something terrible, but we put on a new roof, good for twenty years, and it looks like me and it are going out together.

Our little house burnt down in 1972. We had gone out to eat at the fish camp on a Friday night in late October.

Coming back, we turned left at the store and had gone just a little ways when we saw all the commotion. There was four fire trucks from the Geddie Volunteer Fire Department, which meant that there had better not be a fire anywheres else, and about twenty cars, mostly belonging to the firemen that weren't important enough to ride on the trucks. The Registers, that had been renting the place since June, had burnt it up trying to make a fire. They had to take the seal off the front of the fireplace to even get to where they could start a fire, and when they did, the chimney, full of about ten years of trash and bird nests, caught, which sparked the roof right quick, and by the time the fire trucks got there, it wasn't nothing but a shell, all the windows out and everything all black around them.

We took the insurance money and got out of the rental business. In the spring, we paid Godwin's men to level what was left and haul it off. It's field again now, rented out for hay the last six years, and you couldn't ever tell our little house was there, except for one thing. Right after we moved in, when we was planting everything we could find to make it look less like a field, Sara put crepe myrtles in the front yard because they liked the sun so much. After the house burnt down and we had it leveled, we decided not to plow under the biggest and prettiest one, and when we rented the land for hay, we told the man not to hurt the crepe myrtle, even though it was in the middle of the field. They liked to of killed it twice coming too close with a tractor, so we finally got some landscape timbers and made a eight-foot square around it. That crepe myrtle comes out every summer all pink and beautiful, just when everything else is dying, and it helps me remember what a fine life we had, in spite of everything.

CHAPTER ELEVEN

July 19

Sometimes, when Mom really gets pissed off, when she's really had a bad day, she'll say she has the Sadim touch, like Midas spelled backward. Like everything she touches turns to shit. I think it's hereditary.

Winfrey, Blue and I all passed summer school, and we'd been playing in the Port Campbell three-on-three basketball league for the last two weeks of classes. Winfrey has a car, sort of, a Vega with God knows how many miles on it. The odometer's been cut off for a year, he said. We ride to the YMCA in town and play basketball on Monday, Wednesday and Friday nights. Or at least we did.

Summer school ended last Friday, and Blue and Winfrey both got B's. I got an A and actually kind of enjoyed old *Lord Jim*.

We'd studied together about once a week, and we crammed for the final exam. I don't think either of the Geddies is planning an extensive career in English literature, but they aren't dummies, either.

On the day of the final, I sat in front of Winfrey and beside Blue, to his right, so that either of them could do a little copying if they wanted to. They're not very strict about that in summer school down here. I think they're just happy for any excuse to push people up to the next grade. But the neat thing was, neither one of them had to cheat. On the test we had after three weeks, I could smell Winfrey's breath, and I was afraid Blue was going to tip his desk over from leaning so far. This time, though, I could tell they were doing it on their own. Mrs. Sessoms would leave the room for fifteen minutes at a time, so they had plenty of opportunity, but they didn't need it.

So, last Friday we're feeling pretty good, because we know we're free at last. We have a six o'clock game against a bunch of mean rednecks from south of town, a place called Purcells. They're what Winfrey calls river rats. We'd seen them play before and knew it would be tough. There's this one gap-toothed, red-haired guy, about six two, must weigh 240 pounds, with the most unfortunate freckles I've ever seen. They're dark and the size of dimes. "If that boy's freckles get any bigger," Blue says, "they're going to connect and he can pass for a blood."

The other two players are a couple of squinty-eyed brothers or cousins or something. At least, they look alike. Black, oily hair, dark complexions, jaws like Cro-Magnon man. Their team name, on bright red T-shirts, is the En-Kays, except they spell it "En-Kay's." We're the O's, short for Oreos and less objectionable. I wonder out loud what the hell an En-Kay is. "You don't want to know," Winfrey mutters, and he's looking about as serious as he ever gets, tying his Air Jordans so tight I'm afraid he'll break a lace.

These three-on-three half-court games are pretty informal. There's an official, but you call your own fouls, and he's only there in case of a disagreement. We've been holding our own, winning four and losing one. These river rats, who all play for a school out in the county, are tied with us for second place. The only team we've lost to is the one they've lost to, three guys—six eight, six six and six one—who are returning starters from the state 4-A runner-up at Port Campbell High. They beat us to death, about 120–80, and they probably beat the En-Kays worse.

Winfrey warns me that these guys play dirty, to watch my ass. I've seen them before, and I don't need any warning.

One of the black-haired guys hears us talking and picks up on the fact that I'm from out of town.

"Hey, Luther," he calls to his cousin-brother, "we playin' a Yankee. A Yankee and two Tyrones." Tyrones is what they call black people down here now that it's hazardous to your health to call them niggers right to their faces.

"Where you from, Yankee?" Freckles asks.

I tell him I'm from Virginia, where they actually fought the Civil War instead of waiting for Sherman to come through and kick their butts, and I'm embarrassed that I'd stoop to using that as a comeback. One of Mom's favorite ongoing bitches is what a crime it is for the South to take pride in the Civil War, when they were like fighting to preserve slavery. But Blue and Winfrey don't seem to take offense, and the crackers we're playing just pick up on the Virginia part.

"Whoa!" says Freckles. "We got us a Cavalier."

So for the duration of the game, I'm "Cavalier" instead of "Yankee." Except they say it with a "b" instead of a "v."

The game is pretty close. These guys shouldn't be in our league. Blue and Winfrey are much better players than the guys they're guarding, and even I'm pretty much on a par with the shorter of the look-alikes. But we get rattled, which is what they wanted, I guess. They're slamming us into the walls about three feet beyond the in-bounds lines on drives to the basket, and they call fouls for stuff that's just ridiculous. When we appeal to the official, he's like looking somewhere else. At the half, we lead 42–40 because Winfrey slams one in old Freckles's face just before time runs out. They almost get in a fight over that.

There aren't any locker rooms. We just run to the water cooler and sit on the three rows of bleachers for the fifteen-minute break. I try to calm Winfrey down, although I'm as pissed as he is. He isn't having any of it, though, just sits there glaring across the court at the En-Kays, who are glaring right back. We have a little bit of a crowd by now, with word somehow out that there's scattered unpleasantness with a 60 percent chance of open hostility. The crowd is mostly white, something I haven't noticed before, although the teams in this league are like fifty-fifty.

The Y gym is a little oppressive. It doesn't have air-conditioning, and the heat and additional bodies have taken the smell of the place well beyond the pleasant aroma of sweat socks and Ben-Gay and old wood into the general area of odor. The only thing that saves us from asphyxiation on hot summer afternoons like this is the fact that one of the three doors behind the basket we're using is left open with a piece of wood wedged under it to keep it that way. These are the kinds of doors that lock from the inside when they close, so the one that's open is where most of the spectators come in. A couple of times in the three weeks we've been playing, a ball has bounced outside, gone down the three sets of steps, rolled across the little street out front and wound up in the creek. Winfrey swears that a few years back, a ball with PORT CAMPBELL YMCA stenciled on it washed up at Wilson Beach, down below Newport, and they figured it must have like bounced out of the gym, down the hill, into the creek, then to the river and finally into the ocean. Winfrey's been known to bullshit a little, though.

In the second half, we build up like a ten-point lead pretty fast, but then Blue gets undercut by Freckles going up for a rebound and twists his ankle. Some teams bring along a fourth player, just in case, but we're not smart enough to do that, so Blue has to like limp around in a lot of pain while we let these crackers back in the game.

The official on our half court calls out the time every minute, then every fifteen seconds in the final minute. We play twenty-minute halves. When he yells, "Two minutes," we're tied 78–all. Winfrey calls a time-out, and we sit down on the edge of the bleachers, the six other black guys in the gym standing behind us, either for support or protection. I don't know which. Blue says he can't stay with his man, which it doesn't take Dick Vitale to figure out. I say these jerks can't shoot, so let's like drop back in a zone near the basket, which is what we do. Unfortunately, one of the black-haired guys gets unconscious and hits two fifteen-foot jumpers while Winfrey gets a stickback for us. When the guy gives the one-minute signal, we're down 82–80 and the En-Kays have the ball. They probably could kill most or all of the last minute just holding the ball, because Blue's ankle is getting worse in a hurry, but they think they can toy with us now.

"Switch back to man to man," Winfrey hisses at us, and we do, because he usually knows what he's doing. He and Blue exchange a look I don't understand, and just before the ref calls "forty-five seconds," the guy Blue is guarding goes around him like he's standing still, which he is, and drives for what he figures will be the clincher. At the last second, when it's too late to pass off, Winfrey slides over and gives the boy the most subtle little hip action I've ever seen on a basketball court, transferring all that forward motion into a slant that leads him toward the only opening in the gym. The ball is just leaving his hand when Winfrey gives him the hip. The shot bounces off the side of the rim as the boy goes out the open door. Blue follows the play and kicks the doorstop out. As the door slams shut, Winfrey passes outside to me, I pass back in to him for the slam, and we can hear the missing En-Kay banging on the door from the outside, hollering, "Foul! Let me in, goddammit! The nigger fouled me!"

With the score tied, the other black-haired boy takes the

ball out of bounds. All three of us are pressing now, and he has only one player to pass to—Freckles. To make things worse, Freckles can't decide what he wants to do. First, he bitches at the ref, who has been shielded from the hip action by Blue and me and just wants to get the hell home anyhow. He shrugs and tells Freckles they have five seconds to in-bound the ball. Then he starts counting. Freckles starts for the door, where his other teammate is still banging and screaming, but by the time he gets there and opens it, the count is three, going on four. The boy in-bounding the ball throws it into the crowd to keep from losing possession on a five-second count, and I catch it and lay it in: 84–82, O's. The guy Winfrey pushed out of bounds is too busy getting in his face to notice that the time has slipped under fifteen seconds. Freckles in-bounds to the other black-haired boy, and he throws it back to Freckles, who is Winfrey's man. So Winfrey's guarding Freckles, but the boy he pushed out of bounds is still giving him hell, so it looks like double-teaming in reverse, with Blue not having to guard anybody. Freckles tries to pass back to my man, but he's distracted by the other guy trying to fight Winfrey. So when he does pass the ball, it's pretty easy for me to step in front of the guy I'm guarding and pick it off. I dribble around for the last five seconds and throw up a ten-footer at the buzzer, just for grins, and it goes in, giving me about 10 of our 86 points. Designated white boy, they call me.

All out war is about to break out on the court, with me paired off against the shorter of the black-haired boys. We push and shove a little until this really big black guy, who turns out to be Blue's older brother, grabs me and shoves me out the front door. He's already picked up all our stuff, and the other five black guys there allow us to get out before people start putting on white sheets and burning crosses.

"I was wonderin' when you all were going to get around to using the open-door policy," he tells Blue, giving him and us a smile that, combined with a nose that's like pushed halfway into his skull, is meaner than a lot of frowns I've seen. Nobody, Winfrey tells me later, messes with Blue's brother. His name's Connie, and Winfrey says his friends like to get strangers in bars to ask him what he does. He says Connie puts down his beer bottle, smiles that I'd-be-pleased-to-rip-your-lungs-out smile and says, "I knock suckers *out*!" I'll bet he does, too.

The three of us stop at Hardee's for burgers and fries, then go down to the park, where I get the joints out of my bag. I don't think Winfrey and Blue smoked a lot of dope before I got here, because it really gets to them once they get the hang of inhaling. I brought enough down to get high a little every night for a couple of months, but now I cut back some on personal consumption to share with the Geddies. What are friends for?

Anyhow, we smoke three joints among us, and we are pretty messed up. We're like pumped up over what we did to the En-Kays, and Winfrey finally tells me what En-Kays stands for. Nigger-Killers. This strikes us as so funny that we fall down and start rolling around in the wet grass. Blue forgets he's sprained his ankle until he stands up all of a sudden to go piss. He screams and falls in a heap, and this just makes us laugh that much harder. I almost roll into the river.

We go back to Hardee's for shakes, 'cause we've got the munchies worse than anything. Hardee's, I should tell you, is where the black people hang out on the east side of Port

Campbell. White people hang out at the Burger King up the street. Sometimes, somebody white who's taken a turn off the interstate looking for food will turn into Hardee's by mistake, and it's funny to see how tight-assed they look when they loop around the parking lot and realize that they're in what Winfrey calls the jungle. I just sit kind of low and quiet when we're here. My out-of-town status kind of gives me diplomatic immunity, I guess.

We head out of Hardee's about ten o'clock. I'm thinking that Granddaddy might be worried. He locks up at eleven, and he can't understand what there is to do that time of night that isn't meanness, as he calls it. But he doesn't ride me very hard. He makes me help around the house, and I've cut the grass and picked some peas and beans, although I'm so slow that even he can outpick me. If you do a job bad enough, Trey always says, after a while they won't make you do it anymore. I miss old Trey. I miss old Marcia even more. I sent her two letters; got one postcard that didn't say much.

We take the Old Geddie Road. It seems to me that even the roads are like segregated down here. Black people take the old narrow one that kind of slides down from the center line to the shoulders, which are like eight inches wide, while the whites use Highway 47, which is four-lane almost all the way to Geddie and straight as a string. Old Geddie is where the towns got started, Granddaddy told me. The church there, which looks like a strong wind would blow it over, is the one the white people built right after the Civil War. They sold it to the black congregation a long time ago and built a new one, which looks pretty old to me, nearer to East Geddie. Now, Old Geddie seems to be just about all black, except for this new white housing development called Geddie's Branch that's on a new road running back of the church. Winfrey says they're building a gate at the entrance to it "to keep the natives out."

Winfrey stops at the 7-Eleven where the Old Geddie Road forks off Highway 47, and we all buy Cokes. Winfrey and Blue buy the kind in bottles, so they can hit road signs with them on the way home, which is like a major sport around here. It's not hard when you're sitting on the passenger side, but Winfrey can flip a bottle from the driver's seat over the top of the car going 55 and *whump!* just knock hell out of a sign on the right-hand side.

Tonight, though, Winfrey's a little crazy. As we come up to the only curve on the Old Geddie Road, which has a creek just before it, Blue's already smacked a 35-MPH sign pretty good with his empty, and Winfrey just keeps waving his bottle around and yelling. He almost throws it into a crowd of girls who look like they're walking back from town. When we reach the bridge, which goes over this half-assed creek, it makes that rumbling, hollow sound these bridges make when you drive over them, and Winfrey flings the bottle toward the railing on the left side.

I don't know what happens, but what probably happens is that when Winfrey swings his arm left, he pulls the steering wheel of the Vega with his other arm. Just over the bridge, the road curves right to miss some farmer's cornfield. We go left.

When we leave the road, we clear the ditch in the air, and I guess we'd have been okay, but something's wrong with Winfrey, because we're bouncing along through this field at like 40 miles an hour, except it feels like 100, and he's not stopping.

"Stop, Winfrey! Stop, man!" Either I'm screaming or Blue's screaming, but Winfrey's hit his head on the side of the car or something, and his foot's still on the accelerator. All this doesn't take long, but it seems like forever. They have these big irrigation ditches around here, like Granddaddy's crop ditch, and there's one straight ahead. I'm in the backseat and Blue's on the right up front, what they call the suicide seat, and just before we hit, I duck down, because I don't know what else to do.

The crash is like nothing I could have imagined. When we look at the ditch the next day, you can hardly tell where we hit, but the Vega is, as Granddaddy puts it, "tore all to pieces."

At first after we hit, it's very quiet. I can't figure out what's happening, because I'm looking up at the stars, and my face is all wet. Then I taste the blood. And my nose is starting to ache. I hear voices that sound like they're beneath me. Winfrey asks Blue if he's all right, and Blue doesn't answer. They're under me, somehow, and I can smell this smell like when the hose burst on Dad's car on the way from the beach that time.

Finally, I hear Blue moan, like he's in a world of pain. It feels wet underneath me, and every time I move, Blue moans like I'm hurting him. It takes me awhile to figure out that the front of the car is pointing down and to one side, and I'm looking backward, out the rear window. One back door is up in the air and the other is buried in the ground, so that I can't get to one and the other one won't open.

"I'm sorry, Blue. I'm sorry," Winfrey keeps saying, and Blue's not saying much of anything. I can just barely see Winfrey's face, and it's a mess. He doesn't even seem to see me, he's so worried about Blue. What I finally do is roll the glass down on the low side of the car, the driver's side, and crawl out. I can't breathe through my nose and my head hurts, but it doesn't seem like anything is really wrong. I get Winfrey out through the window, too, finally. He must have hit the windshield with his face, and he's a little out of it. I get him to sit down in the field, right on a corn row by the ditch bank, then I go back to check on Blue. He's all crumpled up on the high side of the front seat, and his leg's bent back. I try to get him to move, but he says it hurts too much. I tell him not to move, that I'll get help. It occurs to me that if the car catches fire, he'll burn to death before anyone can get him out, but I don't mention that and try not to think about it.

I tell Winfrey I'm going for help and head for the road, except I have no idea which way it is. I run through corn taller than I am for what seems like at least five minutes before I get out of that field, and then I can't get anybody to stop. Cars going by slow down, see my face and speed up. The first two houses I go to belong to black people who don't even want to talk to a white boy who looks like he's gone ten rounds with Mike Tyson.

Finally, on the third try, I get lucky. It's this black guy and his family in a mobile home with one of those black-tongued chows on a chain in front. The dog wants me so bad, he's about to pull the metal stake he's attached to right out of the ground. But the guy says, "Hush that fuss, Polly," and the mutt calms down, probably out of embarrassment. I tell the guy what happened and he calls the fire department, which is also like the rescue squad out here. It takes them fifteen

minutes to get there, and it takes us another half hour to find
Winfrey and Blue because, idiot that I am, I forget to make
any note of where we were in the state's biggest cornfield.

They follow the tracks of the car after I finally remember
to tell them that we went off just past the bridge, and when
we get there, Winfrey is like next to the car, talking to Blue,
telling him not to worry and not to die. They get the farmer
that owns the land to get out of bed and open his gate so they
can move an ambulance near the wreck, and by the time they
get Blue out, it must be like two in the morning. They put
all three of us in the ambulance, and when we get to the
hospital, Granddaddy is already there. He looks awful; I
don't guess he's been up this late in his life. Cousin Jenny and
Harold, her husband, are there. They've driven Granddaddy.
He's trying to be calm, but his hands are shaking and he looks
like he's about to cry.

"I'm okay, Granddaddy, I'm fine," I keep telling him,
and he keeps asking me am I sure. All of the Geddies are
there, and they're huddled together on the other side of the
emergency room. They take Blue right in, but it's like
another half hour before they take care of me and Winfrey,
since we obviously aren't going to die. But Jenny and Harold
are after the admitting nurse on one side and Winfrey's
mother is after them on the other, and finally they take care
of us.

It turns out that Winfrey has a concussion and is cut up
pretty badly around his lip and over one eye. I have a broken
nose and a couple of little cuts. After we get stitched up,
Blue's brother pulls Winfrey aside and is talking to him
pretty intensely, and Winfrey is just shrugging and shaking

his head. Blue's brother doesn't speak to me, but he gives me a look that indicates I won't be getting a Christmas card from him this year.

It turns out that Blue has a compound fracture of his left leg, which got pretty mangled when the front of the car crunched into that ditch bank at forty miles an hour. The doctor says he'll walk again, but that basketball is over. They haven't told him yet.

The next day, a state trooper comes by Granddaddy's to get my statement as to what happened. I don't know what Winfrey and Blue have said, so I try to be as general as I can. Then he gets down to it.

"We found a butt from a marijuana cigarette in the ashtray, Justin," he says. He's called me Mr. Bowman up to this point. It's like he's changing gears, like now we can get cozy and talk about what really needs talking about. "To your knowledge, was either one of those colored boys using drugs?"

I give him as emphatic a no as I can muster with a broken nose and six stitches. I tell him that I had never seen either one of them smoking dope. Damn, I'm thinking, I can't believe we left roaches in the ashtray. But I stick to my story, because I'm sure Winfrey and Blue won't waver on this part. Finally, the trooper leaves, but I'm like thinking he might be back. A roach probably won't be enough to convict anybody of anything, but if he can get somebody to say that Winfrey was driving stoned, he could go to jail.

It's just starting to hit me what we've done to Blue. Granddaddy has been very quiet through all this, and especially the part about the roaches. He sees the trooper to the back screen door and watches the black-and-gray car make a dust trail up the rut road to the highway. Then he comes back in the living room.

"Justin," he says, without any beating around the bush, "what's in that green tin box at the bottom of your backpack?"

It never occurred to me to hide it any better than that. Granddaddy doesn't seem like the snoopy kind. But now he's got me, and he knows it. He can probably see guilt in big block letters all over my face.

It turns out that he never opened it. He just saw it there when he was getting my clothes out to wash some of them the first week I was here. I hid the dope box back behind some underwear, and he must have heard it clang when he was moving the backpack around. But I have never been able to lie well, and by the time I know he hasn't opened it, I've already confessed.

"So you got them boys messed up on drugs, and now one of them is ruined for life, is that about it?" Granddaddy sure gets to the point in a hurry, never raising his voice. I try to explain to him that marijuana is like something everybody my age does, and that it doesn't hurt you, but that part kind of gets caught in my throat. I beg him not to tell the police, and he says he won't, but not because of me. He says he'd like to see me spend a few days in jail. Might straighten me out. But he doesn't want "the colored boys" to suffer anymore.

"You've made them suffer enough, I reckon," he says.

So this is like Saturday. I just sit there and he just sits there, me in my room and him on the porch. By midafternoon, it's broiling, but I just don't want to be anywhere where anybody can see me, especially Granddaddy. He's made me get rid of the dope, which I flush down the toilet.

He looks at it, afraid to touch it, like he's seeing the weed from hell. Jenny and Harold come by for a while, but they see that nobody feels much like talking.

Mom's back in Montclair, just flew in on Friday, and she's coming down here for a couple of weeks before she has to get ready for fall semester. I'm wondering how this is going to go over with her. When Granddaddy asks me how I think my mother will feel about this, I swallow the urge to tell him the first people I ever saw smoke dope were Mom and Dad and their friends, when I was a little kid. They quit doing it when I got older, so that Mom's and my dope-smoking days didn't really overlap, at least as far as I know. But I'm not into coke or crack or anything like that, and I never felt like Mom would like slash her wrists if she knew I was getting high once in a while. Until Mark the Narc came along, she took pretty much a live-and-let-live attitude.

Granddaddy says he isn't going to tell her about any of this now, because he doesn't want to upset her before she gets in the car to drive down here. But that doesn't mean he won't tell her later.

I fall asleep on the cot back in my room, and about six o'clock, Granddaddy wakes me up. I'm sweating like a pig, and when I look at my watch, which somehow still works, I can't believe that twenty-four hours ago, Winfrey and Blue and I were just taking the court against the En-Kays. I think again about what Winfrey told me that stood for, and I have to stifle a laugh in spite of everything. Then I think of Blue, and all of a sudden, I can't stop crying. It's the most embarrassing thing, but at least Granddaddy shows a little sympathy.

It takes me a good fifteen minutes to stop, and when I do,

he tells me, "You and me have got to talk. Let's go down to the rock."

So I help him find the truck keys, which are never, ever where he thinks they are, and help him down the steps, which is silly, because he does this like a million times without me or anybody else to help him, and we get in his truck. He drives east down the dirt road and turns left on the trail Kenny took when we went to the cemetery that day. He stops the truck as close to the Rock of Ages as he can get and walks over toward it. I follow.

"You have been careless, Justin," he says when he finally gets his breath and gets settled, leaning back against the rock and looking east, out across the berry fields into the sandhills, which really do look blue this time of day. "This is a good place and a good time to tell somebody, finally, what carelessness can do. And you seem like the right person to tell."

CHAPTER TWELVE

August 8

Nobody knows where the Hittites come from.

Some people claim they was what happened to the Lost Colony, when the white folks went off, or was carried off, and mixed with the Indians. Some say they are descended from Portuguese sailors that come up from Florida even before the English got here, and settled amongst the Indians. Some say they come from thieves and murderers that run off and hid in Kinlaw's Hell and raised their families there. Some claim the first Hittites was Frenchmen that fled their revolution. And some say they come from hell.

There ain't many of them left anymore. Or at least, they have scattered and married outsiders so that you can't hardly tell who they are now. I'll read something in the *Post* ever now and then where some Formy-Duval has been arrested for breaking and entering, or a Boudrow has got married or a Devoe got hit by a car up in Eagle Grove. They seem to be all over the place now. I used to could pick them out walking up High Street when we'd go to town, but now everybody's so mixed up that you can't tell the whites from the coloreds from the Lumbees from the Hittites.

Nobody even knows why they're named that. Momma said they told her that it was because of the Hittites in the Old Testament that the Israelites had to fight to get back the Promised Land. Maybe the first folks from England or Scotland that come across the Hittites was reminded of that story. I'm right sure they had to fight them if they come anywhere close.

We used to have this little song that the boys would sing at recess:

A white man, he shoots with a gun,
a nigger will cut you and run,
a Lumbee will cut you if you look at him wrong,
and a Hittite will cut you for fun.

They was crazy people, and they lived in a crazy place.

If you was to go east from Maxwell's Millpond, you'd finally come to the East Branch, which runs into the Campbell just this side of Newport. Up this far, you can walk across the East Branch just about anywhere, and when you do, you're on the outskirts of Kinlaw's Hell.

The swamp, which is just a part of the Blue Sandhills that's lower than the rest, runs for twenty miles, near-bout halfway to the ocean. It's got bogs and pocosins and about eight billion water moccasins. It got its name because a fella named Kinlaw is said to have walked in there one day to pick huckleberries. He got lost, and was gone for four days. On the fifth day, two boys on a farm clear down at Saraw come across him lying at the edge of the first cleared field on the other side of the swamp.

"Boys," he's supposed to of said, "my name's Kinlaw, and I just been through hell." And when they looked at the back of his ankle, there was this big old cottonmouth that he must of drug for miles. He died right after that. At least, that's the story they tell. It is a scary place. The moss hangs from the cypresses and bay trees, and briars seem like they come out of nowhere to smack you across the face. Daddy got lost in there one time when he was deer hunting, and when he finally got back after dark, one of his eyes was all bloody. It was about the only time I ever seen him scared.

A couple of miles east of the East Branch is the Marsay Pond. There's a paved road in there now from Cool Spring, but back then, a trail was all there was, and folks would get ambushed along that trail. They used to say that the Hittites was cannibals and would put you in a pot and eat you if you wandered over there, but that was just to scare the young-uns, I'm mostly sure.

The Marsay Pond is right much bigger than Maxwell's Millpond, about three miles across. Me and Lafe saw it one time when we was hunting over there, about a year before he died. We come through this clearing and there was the biggest lake we'd ever seen. We'd heard tell of it, but we couldn't believe that this big old lake wasn't but six or seven miles from home and we'd never seen it. And there was little houses, more like huts, built right over the water, so that you could of took a pole and fished right off the back porch. There must of been a hundred of them, all with unpainted boards and rusted-out tin roofs. The water, when we looked down at where it lapped over the white sand around our feet, was dark, like rust or blood, even darker than the millpond. We could see women and children in these little shacks, which was maybe two hundred yards away, but we didn't see no men around. When one of the women that was looking our way started pointing and yelling over to the woman at the shack next to hers, we got on out of there. We didn't want to be anybody's dinner.

The Hittites didn't go to school, at least not back then. They was supposed to, I'm sure, but nobody in the state department of education was crazy enough to go back there and tell them that. They had a funny accent, and when one would come to work in East Geddie at the sawmill, folks would come around just to hear him talk.

The first Scotsmen that come up the East Branch must of been dumbstruck to find all these folks with dark skin and black, straight hair, so black that it looks blue when the sunlight hits it. Some folks called them Blue Hairs. When I hear somebody call a old lady a blue hair, it always confuses me for a second. All the Hittite men I ever saw back then had lean, bony faces, beards and thick eyebrows that met in the middle. They was hairier than the Indians and looked more white, somehow. They said that the Hittites was good-natured folks so long as they wasn't drunk or you didn't upset them, in which case they would as soon kill you as spit.

The women had the same dark complexion and straight, blue-black hair, the same long faces, but on them what was fearsome in the men was real pretty. And Angora was the prettiest one I ever saw.

In November, Daddy would let us have Saturdays off to go hunting sometimes, which was a nice change from cutting ditch bank. That morning, Lafe said he had plans of his own. He had been acting right peculiar, slipping off when we had a free day, or sometimes in the evening, and not telling anybody, not even me, what he was up to. He had got real quiet.

This time, though, I was bound and determined to go with him. I followed him down past Rennie's, across Lock's Branch and into the sandhills. He wasn't too happy about it, but Lafe was too good-natured to stay mad for long.

"Look-a-here," he told me just before we crossed the Ammon Road, "what we do today is just between you and me. You can't tell nobody about this, no matter what."

Of course I told him I'd swear on a stack of Bibles to keep quiet. Secrets was exciting to me back then.

We went across the road and on through the sand and pine straw, headed for the millpond with our Iver-Johnson single-shots over our shoulders, me talking about where we'd seen deer skat in September, him being quiet. It was real warm that day, even for Indian summer, and by the time we had got down to the pond, we was ready to throw our jackets over by the pine tree at the water's edge. It was about eleven o'clock.

Littlejohn

Lafe looked at me right strange, and then he put his fingers up to his mouth and whistled. Before too long, I spied somebody coming out of the woods on down toward the lumber mill. It was a girl, and when she got closer, I could see that it was a Hittite girl. She had that straight dark hair parted in the middle and pulled behind her ears. She had kind of thick lips that made her look all pouty. She didn't seem real enthused to see me.

"Littlejohn," Lafe said, "this here's Angora Bosolet."

I don't know how long they'd been meeting like that, or even how they met, except that her daddy worked at the mill. I never got to talk to either one of them about it. Angora put one of her long tan arms around Lafe, and I couldn't help but wish it was me that she was hugging.

He told her who I was, and then he turned to me and said, "Angora's going to be my wife."

I couldn't believe it. I wanted to ask him what Momma and Daddy would have to say about that, to say nothing of her Hittite family. I asked him when, soon as I got my breath back, and he said soon as he saved up a little money and got up enough nerve. I hate to say it, but I was jealous. I know it sounds peculiar, but Lafe had been the only friend I'd had for most of my life, and now he was leaving me behind. And already I was able to see a world where Momma and Daddy would forgive Lafe for marrying a Hittite, because he always was the favorite.

Angora had a funny accent, talked faster than we did and used her hands and arms more to make herself understood. She had brought a jar of moonshine with her that her daddy had made, she said, and she give us some. Lafe had been drinking for a couple of years, and he'd let me try some of

the stuff one time that the Faircloths sold up by the Mingo
Road, but this stuff that Angora had was different; it would
set your fields on fire. I choked a little on the first sip and
passed it to Lafe, who drunk some and passed it back to
Angora. She took a big gulp and wiped her lips off with the
back of her hand real slow and lazy, and then she smiled at
me and Lafe. I could see what made him want her.

We sat around next to the pond, under that pine with our
12-gauges propped on either side of us, and we passed the jar
around. After a while, Lafe sidled up next to me and told me
that him and Angora was going to go for a walk, but that
they'd be back directly. Said they'd meet me back at the tree
in an hour or so.

He took his gun with him, said he might run across a deer
or something, but I was thinking that it was right unlikely
that any deer in his general direction was in danger of getting
shot that day, the way Angora had her arm around him and
the way they was laughing and giggling.

I felt right neglected, I don't mind telling you. I knew a
little about girls, from what us boys would talk about and
from Alice Fay Cain, who showed me a little about kissing.
But it hurt my feelings to think of Lafe going off with a
woman (although it turned out that Angora weren't no older
than I was, just seemed older) into a whole 'nother world
and leaving me back in that little room at Momma and
Daddy's.

I went down to a place where I'd seen deer skat and
walked around a little bit on the bluff that looked down on
the millpond. I could see the workers over at the mill
walking off in different directions, some up the tram tracks
toward McNeil, some toward the Ammon Road, at the end

of their half day of Saturday work. Down at the other end, the pond looked even more lonesome than usual, with a loon off in the distance making me feel lower than I already did. I took a couple of shots at some squirrels that peeked around the side of a sycamore, but I didn't spy any sign of deer and didn't much care that I didn't, to tell you the truth.

I got back to the tree after one, but they was still gone. Maybe they just won't come back a-tall, I was thinking. Maybe they'll just go off and get married today. I felt like if I could get Lafe back at the house and talk to him, I might get him to change his mind. I wasn't thinking too much about Lafe's happiness.

We'd brought along some dinner. I had a piece of sausage and a couple of Momma's biscuits and then got a drink of the dark millpond water, which you could still do at that time and not die. Then I set down next to that pine tree and dozed off.

The next thing I knew, the whole world seemed like it exploded around me. There was this loud bang and I felt a stinging feeling all over my face. I thought I might be dead, but I didn't know what of. My eyes burned, partly from the sand, partly from looking into the sun. When I was finally able to make heads or tails out of it all, there was Lafe, laughing like he'd just heard the funniest joke in the world. And Angora was next to him, laughing harder than I'd ever imagined somebody that pouty-faced could of.

Lafe and Angora had come back and found me asleep by the tree. They told me that they, meaning Lafe, couldn't help but fire a shot in the sand in front of me just to see what happened.

Now, I take a spell to wake up. I like to of popped Daddy

one time when I was fourteen because he come in and started
dragging me by my foot out of bed, just messing around. You
got to give me a few seconds. Lafe ought to of known that,
but when I saw the empty jar Angora was holding, I knew
that they was most probably drunk. Before I noticed that,
though, I had already made a lunge toward Lafe and tackled
him to the ground. He was still bigger than me, though, and
I come to my senses before I was able to hit him upside the
head with the piece of wood I had grabbed in my left hand.

After everything calmed down, Angora and Lafe sat and
had some dinner. She had brought some smoked fish, which
the Hittites would cook over coals outside and dry out so that
you could keep it a right good spell. Even though I was full,
I tried some.

Angora wasn't talking much now. Her and Lafe looked
over at each other once in a while and kind of smiled, like
they knowed something I didn't, and I felt about as welcome
as a ant at a picnic. But I didn't want to go back by myself.
I had this feeling that if Lafe didn't come with me, he might
never come back.

After a while, Lafe kind of shimmied a little lower down
the pine tree and said he was fixing to take a nap. Sleep it off
is more like it, I thought to myself. But Angora wasn't
sleepy, and she didn't seem to be much drunk. When Lafe
shut his eyes, she started to cleaning up the mess we'd made,
and then she asked me if I'd like to take a walk with her.

"After all, we are going to be family, are we not?" she
said. She had the funniest way of talking I ever heard. I didn't
know what to say, and I didn't know what she meant by
"take a walk." I had a feeling that her and Lafe had been
doing more laying around than walking, from the looks in

their eyes and the pine straw that was still stuck in Angora's hair.

But she was such a pretty girl that she made my head spin. All the girls I went to school with seemed so plain and predictable. Even the good-looking ones was fat with two or three babies by the time they was twenty-one or twenty-two, it seemed like, and you could see them turning into their mommas even before they got out of high school. Maybe Angora had a fat old momma back in Kinlaw's Hell, but I somehow doubt it.

We took the trail that I had gone on earlier, walking alongside the pond on the west side. I asked her where she came from, and she pointed east, over toward the Marsay Pond. She said her daddy, which she called her papa, worked for the lumber mill, and that she would walk with him to work sometimes, and then go fishing in the millpond, which had better and bigger fish in it than the Marsay did, probably because it had better water. The fish that was there didn't have anywheres else to go, since there weren't any creeks feeding it, and they got to be pretty big. It was all fished out twenty years ago, but now they're trying to bring back the bream and perch and even some bass.

I felt a lot like them fish right then, kind of locked in.

She told me that she liked to take water jugs up here with her and bring a bunch back, because the water in the Marsay was bitter and full of iron. I told her about the time me and Lafe had walked to the Marsay and was scared we'd be caught. I didn't tell her about being scared they'd eat us.

"The Marsay folk, we just want to be left alone," she said. She told me a story I hadn't heard before, about when the Klan tried to "straighten out" the Hittites. I didn't know, until I met Angora, that the Hittites didn't call themselves that. They called themselves the Marsay folk.

Anyhow, Angora told me that right before she was born, the Ku Klux Klan got mad at the Hittites because one old boy went back into Kinlaw's Hell to hunt and got beat within a inch of his life. So they figured they'd have a little cross burning right there by the Marsay Pond. Angora said the Hittites let them come on in, down the only trail leading in from the main road, let them set up their cross, everybody with their robes and hoods on, and then they attacked. She said they closed off the only road with a few logs and then they went after the Klan. She said most of the Klansmen went running through the woods after they was attacked by about a hundred Hittite men and women toting everything from tree limbs to knives, and that the Hittites still had horses that was bred from what the Klan left behind that night. She told me that one of the Hittites, a great-uncle of hers, was killed from one of the Klansmen firing into the crowd, and that two Klansmen was killed, one when he got caught between the Hittites and the lake, tried to swim away and drowned, the other one beat to death. She said they hadn't heard tell of the Klan since then, and didn't expect to, neither.

She seemed like she talked more when Lafe wasn't around, and I couldn't help but like her a little.

"Maybe you can come live with us," she said, "after we are married."

We walked on through the woods. All of a sudden, there was a crash in the brush up ahead of us, and this beautiful buck deer, must of been a eight-pointer at least, broke through. The afternoon sun hitting him made him look red.

I was toting my gun, but the whole thing caught me so much by surprise that I didn't even get it off my shoulder. It's funny, but now I can ride up to Montclair and they'll take me for a ride up on the parkway, where we can see deer all over the place. Back then, I probably hadn't seen four live deer in my life.

We stopped and listened to the noise die away. It seemed real quiet all of a sudden, and a wind was picking up. Angora shivered and moved closer to me.

In a day that didn't seem to have no end to surprises, Angora leaned over and kissed me on the cheek. "You are so pretty, like your brother," she said. I wasn't much used to being kissed, and I sure wasn't used to men, and especially me, being called pretty. Then she reached up with one of them berry-brown hands of hers, turned my face toward hers and kissed me right on the lips. I had never tasted nothing so sweet. I was as drunk as if I'd chugged all that moonshine myself.

"We're family now, eh?" she said, and I told her I reckoned we was. And then she laughed like she was dying, like she couldn't stop. I thought she was mocking me and moved away from her, but she grabbed my arm and pulled it around her.

"You English are so funny," she said. That's what the Hittites called us. The English.

It was about two o'clock when we got back to Lafe, and he was still passed out by that pine tree beside the pond. I was feeling my oats pretty good by this time and was still about half drunk from Angora's kiss.

"Look at Lafayette," she said. I don't think I had ever heard anybody use Lafe's whole name before, not even

Momma when she was mad. It always made me wish Littlejohn could be shortened, because it sounded so much worse when Momma would say, "Littlejohn, you come here," than it did when she called Lafe.

"He's still sleeping," Angora said; and then she added, "How good a shot are you, Littlejohn?"

It hadn't occurred to me until she mentioned it, and if she hadn't been there, I wouldn't of done it, because Daddy taught us never to mess around with guns, and I was always more careful than Lafe was.

But here was this beautiful girl, practically daring me to scare Lafe so bad he'd pee in his pants, and the idea wasn't all that unattractive to me, when I remembered how bad he'd scared me when he had the chance.

"I ain't a bad shot," I told her. "Watch this."

I took the 12-gauge, the one I'd got for my twelfth birthday, off of my shoulder, picked it up and aimed. But I didn't aim down on the ground like Lafe did. I picked out a spot about two feet over Lafe's head, right in the middle of the pine tree, so that he'd hear the shot and feel the bullet explode into that tree at the same time. I was about sixty feet away. I could pick off a squirrel at two times that distance.

But then the thing happened that you never can plan for, the thing that can happen when you're careless and don't have no leeway left. Angora, thinking about how silly old Lafe was going to look, I reckon, started to laugh before I even pulled the trigger. It was that same laugh that she had back in the woods, like she couldn't stop. I started to squeeze the trigger at the same time that Lafe woke up, hearing Angora laughing, and saw me pointing an Iver-Johnson right at him. He must of jumped up to try and get away, still half asleep and not knowing anything but that somebody was aiming to shoot him.

He jumped the two feet it took, and the last thing my brother ever saw was me pulling the trigger of my shotgun, pointed at him.

Angora was real quiet for a few seconds. Then she started making this little sound like a hurt kitten. Finally, she squawled like a panther and turned and started running.

Lafe twitched just once. I threw down the gun and walked toward him, and I could see the black blood oozing out of a hole no doctor could ever fix, right over his eyes. Angora was going in smaller and smaller circles, screaming words I had never heard before, some of it not even words. She fell in the sand directly, looked over at me and spit out, "God damn you to hell." She went over to where I was kneeling next to Lafe, just stood there and stared, then turned and started running again, this time in a straight line. I looked down at Lafe, felt one more time for a heartbeat, and when I looked up, she was gone.

A loon cried way off in the distance like a soul making tracks. My last hope was that it was all a dream, and if I started running too, maybe I'd wake up. So I run up toward the sawmill. Even if it is a dream, I thought to myself, I ought to try and get help. By the time I got to the mill office, I was pretty sure it wasn't any dream, but there wasn't nobody at the mill; even the foreman had already locked up and gone home.

I thought about just running into the millpond until the water covered me up, or just heading off into Kinlaw's Hell, never to be seen no more. But I didn't. No guts, I reckon. I run for home. It was a good two miles, but I stopped when

I got to the Ammon Road, thought about running up into Geddie to get help there, or about just turning around and going back into the Blue Sandhills for good, just plowing into Kinlaw's Hell until I disappeared. But I didn't. I kept running for home.

It was late Saturday afternoon. A chill had come up, and the sweat was starting to turn cold under my shirt. I had left the jacket back next to Lafe. I run by Rennie's house, and thought for a minute about just having Rennie and them hitch up the mule and go after Lafe's body, but I could see the house from there, so I kept on going, just slowing down long enough so that when Rennie's brother come toward me, 'cause he could see that something was real wrong, I could tell him Lafe had been shot.

Momma and Connie was in the kitchen fixing supper. I come in by the back-porch door, closing it real careful behind me, I reckon so that there could be one more second of peace before everything ended. Then I turned the doorknob, walked in the kitchen and they both knew something terrible had happened.

"Where's Lafe?" Momma wanted to know before I could tell her anything. "Where's Lafe?" she asked me again.

"He's been shot," I told her, and I couldn't hold the rest of it in. "I think he's dead."

Momma went all to pieces, sat right down on the kitchen floor with the wooden soup spoon still in her hand. Connie said that Daddy was out in the near barn shucking corn. I had run right past him on the way to the house, but I reckon he didn't hear me for the corn sheller, and I didn't hear him for the wind and my own breathing.

So I went out to get Daddy. He was sitting there gathering up corn off the barn floor to shell, and he looked so peaceful there, the old tabby cat sleeping over in the corner. I couldn't hardly bear to tell him what I had to tell him.

"Daddy, Lafe's been hurt bad. He's shot," I told him. He tried to get up quick and fell when his wooden leg got caught under him. I helped him up.

"Where?" was all he could say.

I didn't know which where he meant.

"At Maxwell's Millpond. In the head."

He hitched up the mules to the wagon and yelled for Connie to have the Williamses send for Dr. Horne. Then me and him headed back east to get Lafe's body.

I told Daddy that Lafe had been cutting through some vines when he tripped and the gun went off.

"Don't lie to me, Littlejohn," he said, not taking his eyes off the rut road in front of him. "I can stand anything. Just don't lie to me."

Well, I told him, and it turned out that he really couldn't stand that after all. What I told him, though, was that we was hunting for deer, and all of a sudden Lafe come through some brush to the side of me, and I thought he was a deer.

"Son, how could you mistake your own brother for a deer?" he asked me, like it was a insult to Lafe to do that. Actually, it happens about three times every deer season to somebody in the state. I didn't say anything a tall; the whole idea of what I'd done was starting to sink in, and I started to shivering from more than the cold. I sat there all the way to the pond, shaking. Daddy was crying.

It was just about dark when we got there, and for a

minute, I had this crazy feeling that Lafe was going to pop out from behind a tree and scare us half to death, and we'd all laugh about what a joke he'd played on us all.

But there he was, or his body was, lying right by that pine tree, not moved since I run off, his head kind of twisted to one side. Daddy walked up to him, felt his body and said, "I wish you had of shot me instead."

Then he grabbed his legs and said, "Help me load him into the wagon. He's gone."

He didn't say another thing all the way back to the house, which was where Dr. Horne was waiting, since neither me nor Daddy had told anybody where Lafe's body was.

There wasn't anything to do except have him hauled to the undertaker's, which one of the Williams boys did. I had to tell that story about ten times before they buried him, to every blessed relative that come by, and every time I told it, I could feel Momma's and Daddy's eyes on me, and I knew right then and there that it would take more than one lifetime before they got over it. They might forgive me or at least stop blaming me, but they never would get over it.

We ain't much on sensitive around here, or at least we weren't back then. Times was tough, and nobody thought about sending a boy to see a psychiatrist because he shot his brother by accident. I doubt if there was any psychiatrists around here back then. You was supposed to mind your manners and say yes sir, no sir; be polite and tell the folks how come it was that you shot your brother dead.

"Littlejohn," my aunt Ida, who we saw about four times a year, said, "how in the world did you mistake your own brother for a deer?" And I was supposed to sit there, patient and calm, and tell her how it happened, or how I said it happened.

The worst thing about the shooting, or maybe the second worst, was that, to this day, I can't look you or God in the eye and say, for sure and certain, that I didn't have a little spite or meanness in my heart when I pointed that Iver-Johnson at Lafe. Oh, to be sure I never meant to kill my brother. But maybe I tried to cut it a little too close. If I'd of aimed three feet over his head instead of two, I'd of still missed him a foot when he jumped up. It just shows what comes from going too close to the edge. You can fall off.

I'm only sure that I saw Angora Bosolet two times in my life after that. Both times was within a month of Lafe's death.

There wasn't any sign of her at the millpond, although I reckon somebody looking for a third person could of found them little footprints of hers in the sand, and they might of found the wrapper around the smoked fish and wondered where that come from. But the sheriff was more gentle about it all than my family was, figured that nobody would be stupid enough to lie about shooting his own brother to death because he was a deer, I reckon.

Thing is, I felt like I would be betraying Lafe if I told everybody he was seeing this Hittite girl on the sly, that it would make his whole life seem cheap, like people might snigger and laugh when they mentioned his name. I couldn't of stood that. It seems right crazy now, thinking back on it: I was so concerned that nobody would think any less of Lafe, when he himself was fixing to marry Angora, no matter what anybody thought. I expect that it might hurt somebody a little more to put a bullet in his brain than it would to tell everybody who his secret girlfriend was. But that was the way I felt at the time. Besides, I promised.

It was two weeks after the funeral, walking back from the swamp on a Tuesday, that I seen Angora for the second time. She must of waited until the Lockamys was already headed toward their house, so she could see me alone. We was back cutting the bank by Lock's Branch, and all of a sudden she just appeared from behind the Rock of Ages. I started to back up. It was near-bout dark, there was a cemetery to my left with Lafe's body fresh in it, and a full moon was already up just over the Blue Sandhills, turning brighter by the second.

She looked just as pretty as she did the first time, but she was dressed all in black, and her eyes looked all puffy.

"You've got to help me," she said. "It's your fault. You've got to help me. He was going to marry me."

I turned and run. She chased after me, and for a while, I could hear her feet, near-bout feel her breath as she tried to talk to me while I was running away.

Later, I remember she said something about two months, but it didn't hit me what she meant. I just kind of shut it out of my mind. Maybe if she hadn't jumped out from behind the rock like a ghost, I would of stopped and let her have her say. But I was sure she meant me harm, that maybe she would tell Momma and Daddy everything that happened and make it even worse than it was. Whatever, by the time I come out of the woods next to the Lockamy place, she had give up and gone back.

The last time I'm sure I seen Angora, it was a Friday the week after that. I had to work on the tobacco barn roof farthest from the house, because it had leaked in the fall and ruined some tobacco.

It was a hateful job, because those tobacco barn roofs was steep, and it was a one-man show. I was already starting to talk to Lafe's ghost, and it seemed like any minute I might come over the crown of the roof and see him on the other side, grinning like he did. It made me a little spooked.

I had just climbed down the ladder to take my dinner break when she stepped out of the woods right in front of me. Thinking back, she must of spent a awful lot of time tracking me to catch me with nobody else around twice like she did.

"Please don't run off, Littlejohn," she said, and she tried to smile, but it just scared me worse somehow. "I need help, Littlejohn. Please."

I turned and run. She chased me a quarter mile or so, cussing me and begging me not to run away. But I never wanted to see Angora Bosolet again, couldn't look at her without thinking about Lafe and the millpond.

It was a long time before I found out what Angora wanted. At the time, I thought she was either crazy over Lafe dying, or she was a ghost, or she wanted to make trouble.

The longer I've lived, the more I have become convinced that nothing ever comes to nothing, that everything we do comes back to haunt us, just like Angora did.

CHAPTER THIRTEEN

August 1

Daddy never offers a large opinion, or makes a large decision, unless he feels it's absolutely necessary, that things just aren't going to work out right unless he intercedes. Which is why I am inclined to abide by the wishes of a slightly senile eighty-two-year-old man in overalls who is giving away most of what some would falsely call my inheritance.

Seeing him now, with his short-term memory going along

with his eyes and his heart, fills me with such shame for all the days we could have had together out here on the porch while the sun slipped across one more white-hot summer sky. Even now, though, I can't make myself move back, give up all hope of being a Famous Writer, or even a Famous Scholar, in order to make my own father a little happier for a while.

It was in a little town on the southern shore of Lac Leman that things finally turned to crap for Mark and me.

We had planned our great European tour for months, and Mark had some definite ideas about what we ought to do. He's a newspaper editor, and they can get so neurotic that they make English professors seem like Rotarians. All those deadlines, probably. Mark would try to dole out days in preordained parcels. Get up. Have breakfast (fifteen minutes). See British Museum (three hours). Have lunch (forty-five minutes). Take tube to Hampstead Heath and back (three hours). Stop in pub (thirty minutes). The way I'd always done European vacations, Stop in Pub was pretty much open-ended. I'll give Jeff that; he didn't mind changing schedules if the mood struck him. As it turned out, unfortunately, he didn't mind doing anything if the mood struck him.

We did it Mark's way all through Ireland and Great Britain, from Shannon Airport to the hovercraft at Dover, twelve days of it. I didn't mind terribly much, because I'd already seen most of the British Isles at one time or another, and was getting pretty damn tired of them, to tell you the truth.

Mark would rave on about the English hospitality and sense of order, and those were the things I once admired in the British. But just as good friends come and go but a worthwhile enemy is forever, so it is that the negative things are what stick in my mind: the cabbies calling black people who don't move out of their way quickly enough "Sambo"; the smugness; the black pudding. Anyhow, I like England but do not love her, so there was nothing much that Mark could drag me away from with an anxious look at his watch that I really minded being dragged away from, other than a couple of pubs that needed a pint or two more scrutiny.

But then we were in France, which is what I go to Europe for. We had a small argument before we left about how many days we'd spend there. Mark doesn't like the "Froggies," although he'd been there exactly once, for three days, as part of a seven-cities-in-eleven-days tour. All three days were spent in Paris, and he never got over the fact that the Parisians didn't roll out the red carpet, were actually rude to him. Hell, I told him, the Parisians are rude to each other. Why should they make an exception for Americans?

We agreed, finally, to spend ten days in France, but only if we extended our time in Germany to ten days as well. Mark loves Germany. All that efficiency and cleanliness. The Germans give me the shakes. I can't help but think that the same old guy who's playing in the oompah band was once a young SS officer herding Jews into ovens. But to Mark, the French are more reprehensible for letting the Germans invade their country than the Germans are for invading. The French might be a bit snooty, but they're spontaneous. They will surprise you.

I persuaded Mark to count the day in Zurich as part of Germany, since it's practically the same thing, I argued, and

I would count our day in Geneva as part of France. Montreux and Zermatt we would take from Italy.

So we rented a car and knocked around Normandy for two days, drinking Calvados and eating our first good breakfasts in quite some time. Then we drove to Paris, turned in the car at Charles de Gaulle and took a taxi to our small hotel between the Opéra and Place Vendôme, within walking distance of the Louvre and the Left Bank, to say nothing of several of my favorite restaurants.

Mark doesn't speak French. I speak enough to get by in restaurants and shops and to ask directions on the street—and sometimes understand the answer. The French appreciate it if you try, though. A strange thing: Even though Mark is a demon for punctuality and formality, he never understood about the French and reservations. We would wake up to the breakfast in bed the cheery little maid brought in every morning, we'd eat our croissants and drink our tea, then Mark would leap out of bed and say, "Time's a-wasting," and reel off the nineteen things we were supposed to do before dinner. But what about dinner? I'd ask. We need to make reservations. But he'd hustle me out of our little hotel before we decided where we wanted to go, and then, when we'd stop for a minute to rest our feet on the Champs-Elysées or at the Luxembourg Gardens, he'd be too busy mapping out the next stop to talk about dinner. The English eat to live, he'd say smugly, and the French live to eat. If you cooked like the English, I'd reply, you'd only eat to live, too.

So, we'd wind up about eight o'clock, dog-tired because we hadn't had the afternoon nap any fool knows you need to make the most of a day in Paris, and we'd have to go to a restaurant without reservations. In Paris, you might as well go without shoes. The maître d' of some half-empty eighth arrondissement place would look way down that long Gallic nose at us and either tell us there was no room or make us wait, or put us at the table by the kitchen door. The French are not committed to being churlish. It's just that, given the opportunity and the justification, they're so damn good at it.

It took me until the third day to convince Mark that reservations equated to good manners in Paris, but he sulked the rest of our time there, and I knew he'd spend the next year ripping the French waiters, and the French train stations, and even the fact that they took away the pissoirs, which he'd have bitched about if they hadn't gotten rid of them.

The other bone of contention in Paris was cafés. I was only slightly bothered when we didn't have time to sit and ponder life and darts in British pubs, but cafés are different. I've never understood it, but the waiters in Parisian cafés, especially the outdoor places along those beautiful, tree-lined avenues full of the most interesting people in the world, cannot be persuaded to rush. If you were of a mind to get drunk at the Café de la Paix, you would have to order wine by the bottle. You can sit at the center of the civilized universe for forty-five minutes nursing one Kronenbourg beer and enjoying Paris's best attraction—the people—without anybody asking you if you'd like anything else—like the check—even once. And on the Left Bank, it's even better. They throw in fire swallowers and magicians and the odd street person who'll stop long enough to drink half your beer if you're not watchful. It's slightly more charming than New

York, where the chief attractions are muggings and watching someone go to the bathroom on the sidewalk.

The only time I was able to persuade Mark to stop was at a quiet place near the Boulevard St.-Germain. We'd been there about five minutes when this little gnome who must have been sixty-five at least started talking to us from the next table. He was about five two, very weathered and brown, and he somehow reminded me of Uncle Lex, only much shorter. We could converse well enough for him to find out that we were from Virginia and for us to find out he fought in World War II. Mark didn't know much of what we were saying, only what I had time to translate.

Then the little old man asked if we would take his picture. So I did. Then he wanted to have his picture taken with me; so, with much sign language and flashing eyes, Mark took a picture of me with Henri, which was his name. Then he wanted one of himself and Mark. I had the pictures developed before I came down to the farm, and in that one, Mark looks as if he doesn't want his clothes to touch Henri's.

Finally, he wanted to take a picture of Mark and me, which I thought was sweet. I showed Henri how to focus and where the button was, and he took the camera. He took a step back, then another, on the sidewalk. In the picture he took, Mark seems to have Bell's palsy, because he's in the middle of saying, "The goddamn Frog is going to steal our camera." Henri shyly handed the Nikon back to us. I don't think he heard what Mark said.

We took the bullet train to Geneva for our eighth French day. The last two would be spent on the Riviera, with a friend who has a villa near Vence, in transit from Italy to Spain. Geneva might as well be in France, geographically, but it really has no nationality or night life.

The big thing we had planned in Geneva was a boat trip on Lac Leman, to Yvoire. It takes about three hours to get from the harbor to Yvoire, and there's another boat to take you back every hour or so. I prefer lakes to oceans, and I've always loved the mountains, or at least ever since Daddy first took us the long way back from Atlanta. So, Lac Leman, with these neurotically perfect Swiss towns along the coast and the Alps in the background, met my specifications for perfection. It had been about five years since I'd been near the Alps, and I'd never taken the boat from Geneva.

We sat at a table inside and looked out through the glass at the water and the mountains. Mark had worn only a flannel shirt, no sweater, so that when I wanted to go up on deck, I went alone. We drank Cardinal beer and watched the passengers, mostly Swiss, mostly using the boat as a bus, come and go at Nyon. I wanted to take pictures of some of the children, maybe because they reminded me of Justin, not as he is now, but as he was at five and eight and twelve.

As we got nearer to Yvoire, where we planned to get off and catch the next boat back, it looked as if we were entering the Middle Ages. Everything seemed to have been not built out of stone but chiseled from a solid stone foundation, so that everything—the streets, the dock, the walls and roofs—was seamless. It is one of dozens of such towns I've seen across Europe, planned communities of the Dark Ages, built for common defense and accidentally beautiful, all the more striking because they never meant to be. And Yvoire may be the best of the lot. There were winding streets barely wide

enough for one car; and everywhere there were flowers—
planters in every conceivable spot bursting with a red that
was perfect counterpoint to the austere stone. The town
center's fountain was inundated with them.

"No fair," said Mark, nudging me as we got off the boat.
"We're back in France." He pointed to the DOUANE sign
and perfunctory customs office, and I realized that we were
indeed in that tip of France below Lac Leman. Mark seemed
to be only partly kidding. He was really getting an attitude—
an "attytude" as his mother always said it—about the place.

We walked by a terrace loaded with tables shaded by those
ubiquitous umbrellas that seem to be the premier product of
Europe. I looked at the handwritten menu and suggested that
we take a later boat back and have lunch in Yvoire, with the
lake and the mountains in front of us, the towers and spires
of this perfect combination of French grace and Swiss efficiency behind us. Mark said we didn't have time. It was
approximately the fiftieth time we hadn't had time since we
left Dulles International. It wasn't noon yet, and we already
had a place reserved in Montreux for the evening. I pointed
out that we could probably drive from Geneva to Montreux
in an hour and a half when we got back. I pointed out that
we were almost to summer solstice, that it wouldn't get dark
until after nine.

Mark said we'd get a sandwich on the boat that was
picking us up in thirty minutes. He didn't say we *could* get
a sandwich; he said we *would* get a sandwich. Amazing how
one little word, one little letter, really, can ruin a relation-
ship.

I basically just cleared out a spot there, right on the terrace
of this hotel, and threw a shit-fit. I told him I had passed up

about fifty hours of much-needed pub time, that I had lost a good two days of people-watching in Paris, all because of his neo-Nazi infatuation with making sure the train ran on time. I told him that the train had derailed and it was time to seek alternative means of transportation. It is not pleasant to have a roaring argument in front of foreigners in a strange land. On the plus side, they aren't likely to tell everyone you know about it, but on the minus side, there is this feeling, especially in a tucked-away town such as Yvoire, that you are the sole representative of the United States of America, and that you are making a Bad Impression.

Mark tried to reason with me, but I am not reasoned with easily. Finally, he smiled a little smile and said he was going to wait by the dock, that he had seen enough of France for one trip. I don't know if he thought I would follow him, but when I took his umbrella, which he always insisted on having in case of rain—he wouldn't go to the Mojave Desert without it—and which I always seemed to wind up carrying, and pitched it like a javelin into the little harbor at Yvoire, he might have gotten the message.

I turned to face a waiter with an only slightly arched eyebrow.

"Does madame wish a table?" he asked.

"Mais, certainement," I said with all the aplomb I had left.

I stayed in Yvoire that night, in a little hotel by the water, after spending the afternoon wandering through shops full of lavender and smiles. I had no clothes other than what I was wearing, but somehow I knew that Mark the fastidious would arrange things. So I spent another day in Yvoire, just sitting on the terrace by the lake drinking Kronenbourgs, because it's the only beer the French can make, frankly, and it was beer-drinking weather. I took a nap/passed out in my room in the middle of the afternoon, to wake in the early evening to the smell and feel of a lake in the mountains at the peak of the summer. I felt like Daisy Buchanan.

The third day, I went back to Geneva, all gray, with mist off the Jet d'Eau chilling those of us on deck. I checked at the hotel where we'd stayed and, sure enough, they were holding my luggage. Mark had stuck a letter to the largest piece. It told me where he was going to be, in case I wanted to join him.

I am not made of money; few English professors are. For that, you have to do something really important, such as sell real estate. But I do carry plastic. I rented the smallest car they had for one week, and spent the next seven days wandering through towns between Geneva and the Côte d'Azur. I had dinner in a restaurant outside Grenoble that displayed Alps out every window and had no other Americans inside it. They put a U.S. flag and a French tricolor in a little vase and brought it to my table. I met a Frenchman from Annecy who took me to dinner by the lake there, and I met a wonderful couple at a farmhouse outside Digne when the VW Polo had a flat. By the time I got to Suzanne's, three days before I was expected, I could barely remember Mark's last name.

I never left the boundaries of France for the rest of the trip, until I took the train to Barcelona and realized that Mark and I had assigned seating, right beside each other, for the flight home. We didn't speak all the way back until we were circling Dulles. He asked me if I needed a ride to Montclair, which started me laughing at the vision of myself standing at the airport exit, luggage in hand, realizing I had no way to get home. I graciously accepted. On the way back, we talked, and we agreed to disagree about the way we live our lives. We'll see each other, spend the night together when the miseries get to either of us too much, but we won't be taking any vows, or long trips, together, and that should make Justin happy.

All the trouble my son has gotten into caught up with me several days into the trip, when I called the Carlsons from London. My first feeling was irritation and a belief that he was doing this to make me feel guilty, even ruin my trip. He was so angry about my leaving, and maybe it was selfish, but this was the first time I'd had by myself, away from that town and all our old friends, since Jeff and I broke up.

Then I worried. I wrote cards to him and Daddy every other day, not mentioning the breakdown of relations with Mark, and talked with Justin over the phone. I'm surprised that he ran away, because he's always been pretty close to the vest, maybe too much so, and I'm surprised that he went south, to East Geddie. He and Daddy never seemed to have a lot to talk about, and he was downright rude to Daddy over Christmas.

This probably won't be my turn to be nominated for Mother of the Year, but things have been good between Justin and me since I got to the farm. He's relieved that I don't plan to send him to Fork Union; I'm glad that he took care of his own problem with the English situation. And it seems as if Daddy is a little less disoriented having someone else around to talk to. It appears that they've been looking after each other. Justin can cook a little more than he could when he left Montclair, and Daddy has someone to watch baseball games with on TV.

Littlejohn

It wasn't until yesterday that Daddy told me about the will. He said that I should tell Justin about it myself when we get back, that that was my place. Daddy has always been so careful about not trying to tell us how to raise Justin, always spoiling him rotten when he's down here, but always telling him to "mind his parents," even after his parents lived in different houses and started acting like kids themselves.

Daddy didn't tell me about the wreck until I got down here. Said he was afraid I'd panic and do something crazy. They've set Justin's nose and taken the stitches out, and most of the swelling has gone down. It could have been a lot worse; about the only thing he'll have permanently is a little crease over his right eyebrow that shows when he furrows his brow. A friend of mine in Montclair says that any boy worth keeping will have a minimum of one car wreck before he's twenty-one. I told my friend that that was a sexist statement, that I'd had two wrecks before I was old enough to drink, but now there's a certain feeling of relief that maybe Justin's used up his quota. Daddy said the other boys were both hurt worse than Justin was, and I told him I hoped the driver was, at least. He just gave me a funny look.

Justin went over to Old Geddie late yesterday afternoon, I think to visit with the other two kids who were in the wreck. He walked, and I told him to be sure to walk back, too. Daddy and I ate about 5:30, which is when everybody down here eats. It always takes two or three days for my stomach to get adjusted to East Geddie Time. About 6:15, he asked me if I'd like to go for a ride. I told him fine, but didn't Jenny say that the cops didn't allow him to drive any farther than the Bi-Rite? I told him that that didn't sound like a very exciting ride to me.

"We're going the other way," Daddy said, and after we finally found the truck keys, off we went, by Rennie's old house and the thicket beyond and into the swamp.

I hadn't paid much attention to the Rock of Ages in some time, although the cemetery is right next to it. We used to play down there when I was a kid, although Mom didn't want us to, because she thought it was disrespectful to play that close to a graveyard.

My main memory of the rock, though, is Warren Eccles. He was a senior at Carolina when I was a junior at UNC–G, and I guess he was crazy about me. He came to see me the summer before his senior year, and we put him up in the extra bedroom. It was a horrible summer, with Uncle Lex fading fast, and Aunt Connie dying right after he did. I worked as an intern at the *Port Campbell Post,* and sometimes I'd make up assignments to avoid having to spend part of the night at the hospital with Uncle Lex, or just to get away from all the sorrow. My family is funny about hospitals. If somebody's in one, they feel a moral obligation to have a family member in the room every single minute. When Uncle Lex died, Daddy was right there, at seven in the morning, holding his hand.

Warren Eccles was a brief respite from all that. The only problem was, there was nowhere that we could be alone. He was a handsome boy, about six two, dark, straight hair that he would start growing long by the next fall, although it always looked better short on him; very self-assured, very bright. I wasn't a virgin, and it suited me very well to make love to Warren, but where? Finally, on Saturday night before he was to fly back home, we went for a ride, up to East Geddie, then right on the Ammon Road, past the strawberry patches, and then right again on the old rut road that backs into our land. I had him turn right one last time at Lock's Branch, with the lights off by now, because Rennie was still living then. We made love in moonlight so bright that the Rock of Ages shaded us from it as we looked across the branch at the distant, faint glow of the Blue Sandhills.

Warren and I broke up before Christmas, and he went to Vietnam after he graduated, was wounded and faded from my life. I haven't spoken to him in eighteen years, but he made the Rock of Ages special.

Daddy stopped the truck between the cemetery and the rock. We walked over and looked at Mom's grave, a place I never go unless he wants me to. It's in my will that I am to be cremated and will haunt anyone who goes against my wishes. All this buying flowers to put on an expensive monument to the dead is very offensive to me and serves no one except smarmy undertakers and florists. They are to scatter my ashes off Afton Mountain.

Then we walked over to the rock. Daddy looked out to where the berry fields are, and out across the sandhills, and he reminded me a little of the pictures in my child's Bible of Moses viewing the Promised Land.

"I've made a few changes in my will, Georgia," he said, leaning against the rock for balance. "I hope they won't offend you, and I want your promise, on your momma's grave, that you won't fight it."

And then he spelled out the changes, and told me all, or most, of the reasons for making them.

Justin and I are to get the house and a rectangle of land going north and west from it, about thirty acres altogether, plus money that Daddy has in CDs and IRAs, a surprising amount, really, enough to have qualified him as rich around here, if anybody had known about it. But denying that you have any money is as important around here as having it. I told him that I hoped he spent every last cent of it, because Justin and I are fine, and he probably won't get to take it with him. I only hope it's enough to handle whatever might happen from here on. He forgot to turn off one of the burners on the stove again today.

The land south of the rut road, plus a strip running east from the house to Lock's Branch, goes to John Kennedy Locklear, who Daddy had to explain was the Lumbee who is using a little plot of land back of the garage for a garden. I met him last week, without knowing that he was going to be inheriting about 160 acres of McCain land—and without knowing that he's probably my—what?—stepnephew? half nephew? Anyway, Daddy told me about Rose. He said he wanted someone to know about her before he died. I thought it was a very romantic story, after I recovered from the shock. There always seems to be more to Daddy than meets the eye.

He said he figured Kenny should have the land around the old Lockamy place, since his family did most of the work around here, and that he wanted him to be able to be a real farmer instead of just a practice one. He said that Kenny reminded him of a carpenter without any tools.

The other part is the hardest to understand. Why is Daddy giving the rest of the land—150-some acres, including most of the swamp and the near fields, and the berry patches, which make more money than the rest put together—to a Mrs. Annabelle Geddie, to be turned over to her son, Blue, on his twenty-first birthday? All he'll tell me is where they live and that these are people that we—not he, we—owe a great deal to. From where they live, I deduce that they're black. Is Daddy making reparations? I saw a guy on *Donahue* recently, a really angry middle-aged black man, who demanded, the way that only those who have spent half their lives asking and being turned down can demand, that white people give the descendants of black slaves some unfathomable amount of money to pay for our past sins. It reminded me of when we were kids and we'd try to make up the biggest number in the world, something like ninety-hundred forty-leven triptrillion. Has Daddy decided to try and make his peace with everybody that's been wronged with one symbolic gesture, and are Annabelle Geddie and her son the Chosen People for once in their lives? Or is there something deeper, something personal here? I can remember lots of black Geddies, descendants of slaves owned by my great-grandfather and sharecroppers who worked for my grandfather after the Civil War, but Annabelle and Blue—is that his real name?—are strangers to me. Why did Daddy say "we"?

I have been selfish and self-destructive in my life, sometimes managing the amazing feat of achieving both at the same time, which is somewhat similar to whistling and humming simultaneously. It would be quite impossible, though, for me to do anything else right now other than promise my father that I will not contest his last will and testament. More than anyone else I know, he has earned what is his, and anyone who helped him earn it enough to merit a part of it is dead and gone, as they say around here. The part he's giving Justin and me is a gift, nothing more.

Besides, I sense that he is completely right about this, even if I don't know all the details. He can't remember where he puts the truck keys half the time, and he's called Justin "Lafe" ten times since I've been here, and Jenny pulled me aside before church Sunday to tell me about an incident at the grocery store that is more disturbing than anything I've seen myself. In some deeper sense, though, he seems to be completely in control.

It's funny, considering his lack of education and his generally passive nature—he always let Mom make the day-to-day decisions—but I've never been led wrong by Daddy. Oh, there have been times when I haven't followed his advice, such as when he told me that Jeff Bowman might still have some growing up to do, after we told him we were getting married. He told me I might have some to do, too. Right on both counts, but it took me five years to forgive him and eighteen years to concede that he was right.

The sun is below the horizon, the sky a reflected blue, by the time we finish talking. I help him to the truck. His leg is stiff now, and he asks me to drive back. It is the time of day that sums up all my best memories of East Geddie and the farm, a time when you can drive along with the windows down, your left arm hanging out, and feel a cool relief that seems to spring from the crops and pines and dark, narrow streams. It is a sweetness of high school dates, of hope and promise.

CHAPTER FOURTEEN

August 8

If I hadn't of kept Late's yearbook, I never would of learned more than I ever wanted to.

Georgia was born on December 6, 1947, not much more than a year after we was married. We had planned on having two or three; would of wanted more than that, but I was forty-one already, and Sara reckoned that it would be nice if I didn't have to be pushed in a wheelchair to any of our children's high school graduations. She didn't mind teasing me about being old, because she knew it didn't bother me a bit. I never felt younger in my life.

But Sara had to have a caesarean section, and the doctor told us we shouldn't have any more children. It bothered Sara more than it did me; whenever I'd get a little blue thinking about no little boys to teach farming and baseball to, I'd think of how hard I prayed to God to make her, just her, not even the baby, all right when she was having that caesarean. I had no right to ask for more happiness than He'd give me in Sara.

Georgia was a colicky baby, and with Sara still recovering, I did a lot of rocking and walking at all hours in early 1948. Some mornings, I'd just tell Lex to go on without me, which was about the only day's work I'd missed since I quit school, I reckon. It was Georgia's colic that led me to the one secret I'll die with.

I developed a plan where I would put her bassinet with the rockers on it in front of me while I sat in my own chair in the living room. Then I could just reach out with my foot and rock her to sleep and maybe catch a few winks myself. If she started to crying too loud, so that I was scared she'd wake up Sara, I'd pick her up and hold her in my arms. But I didn't have to do that much.

While I would be rocking Georgia with my foot, it would leave my hands free, and it was a good time to try and improve on my reading, which was near-bout to the first-grade level by now. Anything with words on it was good practice, so I'd pick up a atlas, or a *Farmer's Almanac* or a Bible, anything.

One night, must of been late March, because Georgia was

over the colic by April, I picked up Lafe's senior high school yearbook, which I had toted over from Momma's when me and Sara moved, and started reading every single thing in it, reading stuff about people I had known when we was young-uns. It was still a great joy to me to be able to see anybody's name in print and know it was a name I had heard all my life, to see what Robert Wayne Hairr or Jessie Maxwell looked like in letters.

There was plenty of pictures of Lafe, of course. He was senior class president, and he was in the honor society, and he was on the baseball team—didn't have no football in Geddie back then. Near-bout all the boys and girls seemed like they signed his yearbook. Then I turned to the single pictures of all the seniors, and when I got to Lafe's page, I seen this other picture that wasn't part of the book wedged in there next to his, so that they was facing each other. I reckon Momma might of found it at some time over the years, except I had hid the yearbook right after the accident, because I didn't want anything reminding her of him, and of what I did, like either one of us needed a reminder. And then I forgot it was hid, until we started moving stuff and I found it in back of the plunder room.

The picture was of Angora. It was one of them cheap photographs like people would have taken of themselves away out in the country when a traveling photographer would come through. I reckon one of them fellas was brave enough to go to the Marsay Pond in Kinlaw's Hell.

At first, I was confused. The picture was familiar, right off, but I wasn't sure why or how, and I was about half asleep. It had been more than twenty-five years since I'd last seen Angora, but after the war, it seemed more like a thousand.

I had blocked it out of my mind, I reckon, and the face I was so smitten with that day in 1922 had ceased to be a part of my life. I thought all them years with Rose and all the bad years in the war had wiped that part of my life clean away. Sometimes, though, I think that nothing ever really goes away, that we don't do nothing in our whole lives that we don't answer for one way or another.

When the reason for my confusion about that picture finally hit me, and it couldn't of took more than a minute, I started crying, real quiet so as not to wake Sara or the baby. There are times in everybody's life, probably, when they got it so good that they get cocky and think they don't even need God anymore, that they're one of them "self-made men" that did it all on their own and made their own happiness out of scratch. Sometimes, I think that's the trouble with the United States right now; we got too many self-made men and not enough God-made men. Well, I was feeling right cocky myself there in the early spring of 1948, just back from the war, a pretty young bride and a beautiful baby daughter, until Angora Bosolet's picture popped up in Lafe's yearbook.

I couldn't do nothing about it then but keep rocking and keep crying. What I wanted to do, when I first understood, was jump up from my chair and run out that door, straight east, through fields and the sandhills and on into Maxwell's Millpond until it covered me and my shame forever.

The next morning, I woke up in the rocker with about three hours' sleep, got dressed and headed for the fields. I shook Sara to wake her up so the baby wouldn't be by herself when she woke up, but I was out the door before Sara could say anything to me, or even look at me.

We worked all day plowing. It was one of them windy,

nasty March days where the sand is always blowing in your face and it seems like it's 40 degrees when it's really 60. Every way I turned with that mule, it seemed like I was turning into a hurricane. Spring has never been my favorite season, and this was not going to be my favorite spring by any means.

I had took a sandwich out with me, along with some tea in a Mason jar, and I ate out in the field, blustery as it was. I reckon Sara wondered where I was, but she probably had her hands full with Georgia and figured I just had so much to do that I didn't have no time to come to the house.

After we unhitched the mules, I went up to Momma's and washed my face and hands there. It was about six o'clock, and Sara surely would have supper on the table already. I was near-bout starved, but I asked Lex if I could borrow his car for a spell. He asked me what was wrong with my own car, and I told him it was on the blink, and that I'd have his back to him in a hour or so. He give me the keys, and I got in and headed off to find out what I knew already.

Sara must of seen me go by in Lex's car. There wasn't enough traffic down that rut road for anything to be missed. I turned onto the clay road into East Geddie, then turned right at the store, then left on the Ammon Road, into Geddie itself. When I got to the main intersection, where the Ammon Road becomes the Mingo Road, I turned right on Highway 47, headed east, past the post office and the hardware store and the Southern States building, alongside the railroad tracks.

Mr. Hector and Miss Annie Belle Blue lived on the north side of the road, in McNeil, which wasn't much except two little stores and maybe fifty houses, and the sawmill and lumber company. There had been a post office there, but they closed it before the war. Mr. Hector run the sawmill and the lumber yard; McNeil was where the tram coming up from the millpond linked up with the C&CS line. The main memory most folks would of had of McNeil back then would of been piles and piles of lumber stacked in big yards next to the tracks. It was a place that always smelled like turpentine.

Him and Miss Annie Belle must of been close to seventy then, and they wouldn't live much longer. They hadn't had any children of their own, and it was a surprise to most folks when they decided to adopt when they was in their forties. I could just barely remember them coming to our church with this new baby, and it seemed like they was its grandparents instead of its momma and daddy. But they had it better than most around here back then.

Mr. Hector didn't have to worry none about bad weather or the low price of cotton, and the house they lived in was theirs for free as long as they wanted it. It had been built by a great-uncle of Mr. Hector's, one of the McNeils that used to own most of this half of the county, and was fancier than most of the houses around here, made out of brick with little round windows on both sides in the front and a gazebo in the back yard. Unlike us and most folks around here, the Blues had a lawn instead of a yard. All we had to do to clean our yard was sweep it with Momma's broom and pull up the weeds that come up through the sand. Mr. Hector had to hire somebody to come in with a push mower to keep the grass he planted nice and even. He started a trend, and by the time Lex and Connie died in 1968, I was spending four hours every two weeks mowing the centipede grass Momma and Sara set out in 1952. Folks all over town would tease Mr.

Hector, telling him that he cost them fifty extra hours of work a year. He'd just smile and tell them that if it wasn't him it would of been somebody else, or he'd tell them to just buy some concrete and green paint from the Godwin Lumber Company, cover over their yards and paint them green. Even offered to give them a discount.

I reckon that Mr. Hector knew I had something other than building supplies on my mind that evening. It was 6:30 by the time I got there, bumping over the train tracks in their long front yard and looping around to the back of the house on their circle driveway.

Mr. Hector was out feeding table scraps to his beagles. It was near-bout pitch dark, and the wind had died down some to where it felt right pleasant for the first time all day. He said that him and Miss Annie Belle had just finished supper, and wouldn't I come inside and have some banana pudding that she'd just made today.

"Mr. Hector," I said to him, "we got to talk."

He could see that I didn't mean inside, so he motioned me over to the pumphouse, where we both could sit, not looking at each other like we would of at the gazebo. So we got settled there at the pumphouse, our feet not quite touching the ground, and I asked him what I had to ask.

"Mr. Hector, I know you probably don't want to tell me, but I got to know who Sara's real momma and daddy was."

I could hear the dogs snuffling around, giving out a little yelp now and then when one thought he wasn't getting his share, and I could hear Miss Annie Belle clinking things together in the dishpan through the half-open kitchen window.

"I oughtn't to tell you that, Littlejohn," he said. "I

promised that I never would tell, and I don't see what earthly good it would do now. I sure don't think she'd want to know, and I don't reckon you do, either."

"It ain't a matter of wanting to know, Mr. Hector. I've got to know. I can't rest till I do."

I promised him that I would never tell another living soul, and especially Sara. They'd always told her that she come from a orphanage, and that seemed right to me at the time. But now I had to have the truth, no matter what.

Later, after he had told me everything, I went on home. Mr. Hector was concerned about me never telling Sara. If he had known the whole story, he wouldn't of had a care in the world about that.

Sara wanted to know where I'd been. I said I had to talk over some business with her daddy. She said what business, and I told her it was a secret. She kept after me for months to tell her what me and Mr. Hector talked about that evening, but I never did, and it hurt her feelings. It was about the only thing we never talked about. It's a great open hole in my life now, not having Sara here to talk about things with. Nobody, not even your own child, is as good for that as your wife is. But I couldn't tell her. She might of hated me, or felt like she had to leave, and I couldn't of stood that.

First chance I got, I burnt that picture of Angora in the oil heater.

Mr. Hector said that one evening in the late summer of 1923, him and Miss Annie Belle had just finished supper and was out on the porch, fixing to take a walk before it got dark, when a man come to the back door. He had a burlap bag with him, throwed over his shoulder. Mr. Hector recognized him from the mill, said he'd worked there for about three years.

The man wanted to talk to Mr. Hector alone, but when he saw what was in the sack, Mr. Hector fetched his wife. What was in there, wrapped in a diaper, was a baby, although she didn't have no name a-tall then. The man said him and his wife had been keeping the baby since it was born, two months before, but that his wife said that she was through raising young-uns, and that if he didn't do something with this one, she was going to wrap its head around a pine tree, just to keep it from crying.

It turned out that the man's daughter had had a baby out of wedlock, and then had run off the week after and hadn't been seen since. They didn't even know who the daddy was, and the daughter wouldn't tell, no matter how much they beat her.

Mr. Hector said they took the baby because they was afraid that she wouldn't live long enough for them to think about it. He said he told Miss Annie Belle that they could always give her to a orphanage if it didn't work out, but that after a few days, there wasn't much doubt in either of them's minds that she was a gift from God. They had a friend, one of Miss Annie Belle's cousins, that was a doctor, and he took care of getting the baby's birth date postdated. They reckoned that she was born two months earlier, so it went in the books as June 23, 1923, and they named her Sara Joy Blue.

Mr. Hector said the man that brought them that burlap bundle was a dark-haired, bushy-browed man, fearsome-looking, and that he worked at the sawmill for two more years and never once gave any sign that he had ever seen Mr. Hector except at the mill.

He said he couldn't remember his name, but that he had

all the pay ledgers for the past thirty years in his office. I asked him if we could see them right then. He looked at me right queerly, but he got his flashlight and we walked across the road to the office. He finally found this dusty little ledger book marked "1923" and went down the names on the payroll.

"Here it is," he said directly, his bony old finger stopping halfway down a column. "Marcus Bosolet."

I had always believed in God, in His wrath and mercy, but ever since I found Angora's picture in Lafe's yearbook and knew who her daughter was, I have continued to be confused as to His intent. Was He punishing me for Lafe's death by arranging it so that out of all the women in the world, I would fall in love with my own brother's daughter? Did He mean for me to leave her when I found out the horror of what I'd done? Or was I supposed to look after the truest victim of that shot from my Iver-Johnson 12-gauge by giving her a happy life? I prayed for months, asking for a sign. The only sign I ever got was an ever-deepening love of Sara and Georgia, until I finally told God that if He wanted me to turn my back on my sin, He would just have to damn me to hell, because I wasn't going nowhere of my own free will. But I did ask Him to help me keep this shame from Sara, and everybody else, and just let me do the answering for everybody. So far, I reckon He's cooperated.

And so, Angora never left me. Every time I looked at Sara after that, I could see her momma's wild beauty, and more than a little bit of Lafe, too. I could understand then why I'd fell in love with Sara. As for Angora herself, I never tried to find her, because she was the one other person that could spoil everything, the whole life we had in East Geddie. But I'd have nightmares where she showed up at our back door, looking just like she did the last time I seen her, crazy-looking and begging for help, and Sara would ask me why I was turning her away, somehow not seeing that Angora looked just like her.

Twice after that I thought I saw her, and that she saw me. The first time was at the tobacco market in Sampsonville in 1955. I brought Sara along, just to break the monotony, hers and mine. As we was sitting in the hot pickup truck, drinking Coca-Colas and waiting our turn, a woman walked toward us, on the other side of the street by the tobacco warehouse, and looked right at us in the cab. When she smiled, I could of sworn that it was Angora, who would of been near-bout fifty then. But she just kept walking. I looked in the rearview mirror and she had turned half a block down the street and was looking right at my eyes. I held my breath for a second, then she turned around and kept on walking. I have to admit, I didn't mind missing them trips to Sampsonville after we turned to raising strawberries.

The other time, it was 1962, and I was shopping at Belk's in Port Campbell, looking for a Sunday shirt. I looked up, and this old woman was looking at me through the front glass of the store. She looked more like seventy than the fifty-five or so Angora would of been, but it favored her enough that I threw down the shirts I was looking at and walked out of Belk's the back way.

For years I've looked at the obituaries every day in the *Post,* and I never have seen her name. I've seen two Angoras, one of which might of been her, but probably not, and a handful of Bosolets. A cousin of hers one time wrote a check for strawberries at the shed. I seen the name and asked him if he knew Angora Bosolet. When he told me she was his fourth cousin, I asked if he knew what had become of her. He said he didn't know, that she run away a long time ago, and that he'd heard that she turned out bad. That's all he would say. He asked me my name—I reckon he figured I just worked there. I made one up.

CHAPTER FIFTEEN

August 8

I wake up, and it's cooled off.

It looks like the Lord wants me to go on living, for some reason. I feel right light-headed, and I wait a couple of minutes before I try to raise myself up off the little stool. It must of clouded up, because I don't see any shadows, but everything looks bright, like the sun is shining just back of the clouds and making them glow like sunset.

I'm wondering how come the weatherman didn't tell me nothing about this cool front a-coming in when I look over and spy that pine tree. It's as big as it was in my dream, two hundred feet high at least, and six feet across, biggest pine I ever saw. And out from behind it steps Lafe. He's nineteen again, skinny and smiling, with his red hair all mussed up like it was most of the time. He's got a scar over his right eye.

Lafe don't say a word, just motions to me, and I don't seem to have no voice right now. I get up, easier than I've got up in years, don't even need my cane. Lafe is walking out toward the millpond, which is clear and blue now, like the water has been purified. And then he's in the water, except he's not really so much in it as on top of it. I'm supposed to follow him, but I still remember my dream and I'm still wondering if this is another one. Lately, it's got harder and harder to tell what's dreams and what's real.

Finally, he's about a hundred feet out in the water, and he turns around again and looks at me, just looks and don't say a thing, but it's like my feet have a life of their own, and they start moving toward him, toward the pond.

The water isn't even getting my feet wet. I'm out several yards and I look down and see that I'm just walking across the surface. Lafe somehow makes me understand that I'm supposed to look up. I do, and he nods and smiles, makes a forward motion with his hand and I follow him. That old hymn we used to sing at church, "Walk on Galilee," comes into my head, the one that had the chorus that went:

You can walk on Galilee,
Cross that shining, peaceful sea;

Littlejohn

If you put your faith in Jesus,
You can walk on Galilee.

Now I'm out where the water ought to of been over my head, but it's like walking on glass, except different, because this feels more like feathers. Lafe points on up ahead, and I can see where we're heading to.

There is a mist now, making everything hazy and hard to see, except out in the middle of the pond, where the sun seems like it has broke through and is shining on a whole bunch of people. It's just like in my dream, only prettier even. There's Momma, looking like she did at maybe thirty, still in good health and smiling to beat the band, happier-looking than I've ever seen her. And Daddy, with the twinkle in his eye he'd get when he would tell us about the war and all, but looking younger than I ever saw him, a lot younger than he was when I was born, I reckon. Him and Lafe don't look like they're father and son, but more like they're brothers, both with their wild red hair and long, bony faces. I can't figure out how they can all be so clear to me, because they're smack in the middle of the pond, must still be a quarter mile away.

I see Angora and Rose, standing side by side, with their different kinds of dark complexions, both looking as pretty as they looked on the prettiest days of their lives. They're waving at me and motioning me like I ought to hurry up, or like they can't wait to see me. And I see Lex and Connie and Century, not that long gone from my memory, all looking like they're young-uns again, or in their twenties anyhow, and they look like they might be getting ready to start a game of run-cat-run.

I think about the time that Georgia and Jeff took me to see a play that the college was putting on. It was a terrible sad one, with everybody just tore apart at the end from what they had said and done to each other, and I wondered why anybody would want to watch something that made you feel that bad. And then the curtain went down and came up again, and these same folks that was destroying each other just a minute before was all smiling and bowing, with their arms around each other like they'd been best friends for life. Was we all just play-acting?

Back behind the rest, a little higher up, is my Sara. She has her hand on Angora's shoulder, in a way that tells me somehow that they've found each other and know everything. Sara is even prettier than her momma, as pretty as she was in the parking lot of the Geddie Presbyterian Church when she first let me know that she cared about me, with her dark hair and flashing eyes, misted over now with tears like mine are. She holds out one tan, thin wrist, one of the wrists I used to love to kiss when I'd wake up in the morning with her curled beside me in our feather bed, and I feel like I won't be able to stand it if this is a dream and I have to wake up old and crazy.

I'm not more than a hundred yards away when I catch up with Lafe. I put my arm around his waist and he puts his around mine, and we walk toward the light.

This time, I won't look down.